THAT'S LIFE:

ARLISSA'S
Encore

GODDESS A. BROUETTE

THAT'S LIFE:

ARLISSA'S

THERE ARE NO HEROES HERE.

THAT'S LIFE:

ARLISSA'S

This book is a work of fiction. Names, characters, places, and incidents are the product of the author's imagination or are used fictitiously. Any resemblance to actual events, locales, or persons, living or dead, is coincidental.

Cover Design | Editing | Book Design and Typesetting
Enchanted Ink Publishing

ISBN: 978-1-7374147-5-9 (E-book)
ISBN: 978-1-7374147-4-2 (Paperback)
ISBN: 978-1-7374147-3-5 (Hardcover)

Thank you for your support of the author's rights.

Printed in the United States of America

Inner
Child
Publishing
SINCE 2021

This book is dedicated to my Godmother and Godsister, Kashola and Ashley. It is also dedicated to my cat, Tom. Thank you for the priceless love, confidence, and support that you instilled in me.

TRIGGER WARNING

While I enjoy writing dark fiction; the tones, themes, and events can be quite triggering. Please be cautious of the following triggers that are included but not limited to: mental illness, grief, death, physical and mental abuse, and addiction.

GODDESSABROUETTE.COM

Prologue

Standing here isn't on my "Things to Do While Pregnant" bingo card. Paparazzi shielded themselves in the bushes but jumped out when they caught wind of me. It's like they knew. Or they were waiting for Alejandra's outfit of the evening and got lucky. Ha, lucky with me? A picture of me wouldn't sell for a dime these days. Not anymore.

I was almost there—nine months of pure isolation, and no one had a clue. My name blessed headlines without fail for the first four. If I was papped going to the store, the world would suddenly remember me. I'd have to shut off my phone for another three weeks and pray the Twitter threads don't bombard my feed when I return. Return on my burner account, of course. I deleted the real Arlissa Benson accounts as soon as I could. The theories, the thoughtless opinions, the fucking stans. When are they going to realize that hashtags don't save lives?

No one knows about my baby, though. No name. No gender. No identity. Do I even know about my baby? Yes. None of that makes it any less real. Thankfully, I'm gifted with barely showing. Thankfully, no one wants anything to do with me anyway.

The paparazzi snapped a few pictures. I remember seeing the flash in the corner of my eye. Xavier's hoodie did the trick of hiding what I've kept to myself for so long. But the public's opinions and conclusions are out of my control. Maybe that's why she let me in.

"I didn't want to fucking lie to you! It just happened!" I blurt out in a desperate attempt for her to hear my side.

"Oh, it just happened? You just happened to jump on the dick of the person I was in love with for-fucking-ever?"

I roll my eyes. God, I wish I was arguing with anyone else. "For fuck's sake, Alejandra, you're married! How long is forever to you anyways? It was high fucking school!"

Alejandra is always dressed to a ten, even when you barge into her home in the middle of the night after not seeing her for months. I tried; I swear I did. But I simply couldn't bring myself to text her. And even when her dark hair is tied together by a single clip and the makeup of the day is halfway gone—she's stunning. With pain and disappointment painted all over her face, how could I not feel like absolute shit?

"Just because he wasn't the one doesn't give you a right! Have you lost your entire mind? Like, hello? Is anyone home in there?" the woman shouts, and her gold robe flows behind her while she stomps to the front door. Even looking through the Sunday paper. "Oh God, are you bleeding on my floor? Is there any way you can just—plug it up?"

"Do I look like I can plug it up?" I snap.

She raises her brows in annoyance and reaches over to shut the water off. "Come on, get in." Her hand reaches out to mine, and she assists me with not falling headfirst into the tub. *If you don't do anything else right now, Lissa, advocate for yourself. You got this, baby sis.*

The hoodie increases in weight as the thread gets soaked with water. I quickly try my best to pull it off and toss the substantial fabric onto her floor. At least that will soak up some of the blood she's so worried about. I kick off my underwear as well and avoid any awkward looks from Alejandra that I know for sure are coming.

Please come out. Please just make this one thing easy on me.

"Oh . . . Oh gross," Aly whimpers with one eye open. "The head . . . Oh! Google says that means push." She stays near the door in case she needs to run out at any moment. The water turns pink from the blood, and I begin to take her advice.

I can't live without this baby. Without the last physical reminder of Xavier, I'll have no one. I would have lost everything for nothing. I want to call my mom, but I can't—fuck!

This baby feels like it doesn't want to come out, but I keep working with it. I push; I ignore the fact that Alejandra is pacing around the bathroom like she's the one giving birth, and I push.

"I think I need to grab its head," Aly mumbles, disgust coating her words.

"So do it!" I shout while gripping tightly onto the porcelain that I'm currently encased in.

Aly hikes up her nightgown and takes a deep inhale before shoving both hands into the water. "It's fucking slippery!" she shouts, so I push once more to make it a bit easier.

It still hasn't done the trick. I look down at the chaos and give it one long push until half of its body feels like it's ripped me open, and Alejandra is able to gently tug the rest out.

"The cord's around her neck!" Aly shouts at the same time she's removing the child from the water. She hands her to me, pulls open one of her many drawers in this bedroom-sized bathroom, and grabs a pair of scissors. I'm barely here, unsure exactly how to feel or what to say, but there's a baby in my hands and she's not moving. Like she's done this before, Aly cuts the cord, and instantly a roar of cries comes from the baby's mouth.

I stare down at her, a baby girl that I know I deserve. I kiss her forehead and allow myself to just breathe for a second. But something still doesn't feel right. My eyes wander up to Alejandra, who is slowly backing away from us.

"Thank you," I whisper pitifully.

"Sure as hell hope you didn't kill him now." And that's it. She quickly turns and closes the bathroom door behind her, and what should be celebrated is quickly tainted by the reality that shit still sucks.

Chapter

ONE

*L*ast July wasn't the worst day in the world; I know that much. But today? Well, today definitely is. Happy death day, Xavier. I'm going to trial.

"You're like a modern-day Marie Manning! Look, look! You're trending number three right after 'Aquarius.'"

"Who the hell is Marie Manning?"

Madison scrolls, in his own world. "Hm. I wonder why Aquarius is trending."

"More like a modern-day Lucrezia Borgia . . ." Evelyn mumbles from the other side of the limousine, her gaze not even bothering to rise from her phone screen. I wonder if it's because she's on Amy's payroll or what, but Evelyn has been a bitch since I met her.

"And who is that?" My voice jumps a little more, but still, no one is answering my questions. "Regardless, I don't want that. I want a medium vanilla frappe and to be home instead of on my way to have total strangers decide whether or not I killed a man while another woman is at home doing my job."

There isn't an immediate comeback. Just uncomfortable, tear-jerking silence.

"Never mind that, look! Everyone is talking about you. You've stolen the show without even stepping out of the car."

I sigh, leaning over just a bit in order to look at the man's phone.

#Aquarius

#Arlissa Benson

#NFT

#Justice for Xavier

#MDF 50th anniversary

#Savannah and Aly

My eyes immediately escape from the screen, focusing on the shiny leather in front of me instead. "Can we talk about anything else other than my name in people's mouths who have never even had a conversation with me?"

We both choose to ignore the last few trending topics we accidentally stumbled upon. "No one has had a conversation with you in a year. Maybe that's the problem."

"No one has had anything valuable to say in a year," I shoot back. I'm tired of this same conversation. I can feel it coming. It's the way the gray in his eyes gets covered by black when his pupils dilate. Or the way that awkward smile stays plastered on his goofy-looking face whenever

there and tell you about the person—the brother—that he lost. He's going to tell you that it was a night like any other, a night where he hung up the phone on his best friend and did not expect that to be their last conversation. How he didn't expect the last time he got to hold his old roommate would be at his open-casket funeral. You'll hear about his wife, Alejandra Garcia, and how she aided him through the last year."

Go ahead, look down. You got it? Let the camera know that you feel his pain. Let them think that the name Alejandra Garcia still means something to you.

"He's going to tell you that when he laid down with her that night and shut his phone off, he didn't expect to be awoken by the rush of police and EMTs in the hallway. He will speak of his best friend, the terminal relationship he saw him in, the way his smile lit up a room when he spoke about something passionately, how he loved the people around him, and most importantly his cherished character. Because Xavier Amari wasn't only an undefeated boxer but a friend, a lover, a philanthropist, and most importantly a son who wanted nothing more than to be a father before twenty-five."

Breathe. You stopped breathing.

"Greyson is a very deep sleeper. You'll find that he had the ability to sleep through whatever commotion was going on in the condominium upstairs. He was shaken out of his sleep by his wife screaming that they needed to go help. Help with what? He wasn't sure, until she insisted they get an Uber instead of driving—he saw the first responders and the cop cars. But he still had hope that his best friend was fine."

This is a sob story. An exaggerated, unnecessary sob story. No one felt bad when he was clouding up my mind and ripped my tops off because he simply didn't like them.

"Several doctors rush through the halls, none of which are assigned to Xavier, so they wait some more. They watched and waited patiently because someone had told them that he was in the room right down that hall." She's talking with her hands now. Her brown eyes are locked on the jury as if they all forgot I'm even here. "Finally, it's the childhood best friend of this sports superstar who gets up and demands answers. And to the family's surprise, Xavier had been pronounced dead at the scene. His body hadn't even been brought to the hospital yet."

No one felt bad when I was shaken out of my sleep because he was losing an inner war with himself—all the fucking time. I was supposed to be there. I was supposed to be his partner, his support system, his therapist, and another name in his hat of bragging rights. I wasn't supposed to be my own person. Not with him.

"He was now a full hour away from his best friend, who was now getting transferred to God knows where. Eventually, he ended up going from the hands of the woman he loved to the gloved hands of an MD recipient with a cold scalpel. It wasn't until hours later from a celebrity gossip blog that they learned the horrifying nature of their loved one's injuries. And you will hear from Dr. Lawrence, the coroner who received Mr. Amari's cold body. She examined the gashes, found the pills in his system that caused him to sleep so deep that he wouldn't react when his wrists were viciously ripped open."

I have felt my grief, my weakness, and my fear. I have felt compassion, understanding, and stupidity. I have felt it all down to the nitty-gritty falsified sense of guilt. Now? I feel rage. Disgusting, mind-boggling, embarrassing rage. If anyone deserves a fucking memorial, it's me.

"Now, if we go back to the defendant, Arlissa Benson, who did this. She decided to begin a relationship with a man who she knew had a lot on his plate. Constant criticism from friends, the public, and colleagues. A constant pressure to be perfect and never lose anything at all. A relationship history that was wide open for the entire world to see. Xavier Amari wasn't allowed to grow in peace, but she was. And still, as she sits here today, she is allowed more than Xavier ever was."

Don't look down. Don't look disinterested. And goddammit! If you do nothing else, Arlissa, you do not look defeated.

But no one picked my side when the doctors could clearly tell that the fractures in my skull weren't from falling down the stairs. They won't keep taking away my pride. I won't allow it. Not this time.

So fucking look up!

The judge finally shuts it all down, chiming in like an angel I never knew I needed. "You may call your first witness."

"The state calls Greyson Moore to the stand."

This is going to be a no-brainer. I know that much. The man hasn't had a single independent thought since I met him. Xavier's party. September 2017. My first time in LA, and I was driving a car with an engine that roared louder than Aly's stomach on Taco Tuesdays. Somehow, she married the guy who I found nose-deep in cocaine and girls the first night we met. Somehow, she's the happy one.

Stop thinking about it.

Greyson adjusts himself at the stand, attempting to find comfort in an uncomfortable situation. I can see him struggling, so much so that he might break his brain. Thick brows remain furrowed as he places his right hand on the Bible. Even though he seems to be participating, he's using his left hand to scratch the newfound scruff that's wrapped around his chin and jaw. He's always been attractive. A quiet idiot. Always blending in with the scene and wearing whatever he felt would make people respect him more. Yet there was never anything respectable about him. Just a thoughtless lapdog to whomever needed one.

That's my best friend, you know. Calm down.

Look at him. He's fucking sweating. Everything has always been a game to him. He has his suit and tie, trying to look all smart and shit.

But not too smart. Not smart enough to threaten anything said by the prosecutor, you know that. He's close to my family. Don't underestimate him.

Fine.

I almost lean back, but I know the cameras are still analyzing every move I make. I look relaxed? I'm not taking this seriously enough. I lean too forward? I'm scared because I'm guilty of something. Let's find a happy medium.

Prosecutor Mara Baker, the woman who doesn't even have a better-looking pantsuit than me, is supposed to intimidate me? Yeah, we'll see.

The judge looks down at him as he nervously tugs at the sleeves on his black suit. "Good morning, Greyson."

"Good morning."

Mara interrupts. "Good morning. Would you mind turning to the jury and introducing yourself?"

The younger male leans into the microphone, his normally tan skin going completely pale. His hazel eyes are twinkling under the dull lights. "Yes, ma'am. My name is Greyson Moore."

I remember Aly's Halloween party, the first time we ever had a full conversation. I remember wondering if I was steering clear of him, or was it he who was steering clear of me the entire time?

"What's your occupation?"

"Brand owner and public figure."

"How long?"

"Since I could use the internet." Bragger. "But my clothing line is a few years old."

"And did you start this clothing line alone?"

"No, with my best friend, Xavier Amari."

"Can you briefly describe your experience starting this business with him?"

He gulps hard. I can see it from my seat just as clearly as I can see the beads of sweat on his forehead that his brown hair is desperately trying to conceal. "He was excited. I mean . . . Xavier accomplished a lot for anyone our age. He was only—" He pauses, squeezing his lips tightly together in a desperate attempt to go on.

"Take your time," the judge whispers.

"He was only twenty-four, you know? And whenever he talked about anything he was passionate about . . . like sweatsuits and baseball caps, he could talk about it all night."

That's because he was on coke.

"How long did you know Mr. Amari?"

"My whole life. We went to the same schools, played the same sports. Our families were in the same social circles." Regardless of the clear fear smeared across his features, everything he says comes out as if it were rehearsed.

"And how would you describe him in general? If you wouldn't mind. I know this is probably still very hard for you."

Greyson sits up as if he had been waiting to talk about this for the last twelve months. "I didn't know family could be more than blood before I met him. I didn't know how

24

to recognize it at least." A light chuckle bounces off of the microphone as he tries his best to remain composed. He avoids me now, looking instead for any cameras in the room and focuses on those instead. "When we met, we were just kids fighting over who had the better Pokémon cards—it was always him. Ha, he always won everything. As a kid it was annoying, but as an adult it was admirable. Xavier grew up before the rest of us. He had to. His parents had high expectations for him, but that didn't stop him from giving me the shirt off his back if I asked. And trust me, there were times where I had to ask. I mean, the man hosted parties so stressed-out teens had a place to cool off."

Or do coke in his bedroom.

"He gave rides to people who needed it in high school even though he didn't have to and had to get to practice or do something with his dad. No matter what, he always fit others in. He didn't deserve what happened to him, man." Greyson gulps again as his hands begin to tremble. "We actually shared that condo, you know? That he, uh . . . And I never thought it would become his coffin. No one who knew him did. And listen. I know you will hear that he had issues, and who didn't? In our position, it's hard, man. I can't mourn in peace without someone asking for a statement. He couldn't even go through a breakup without unwanted opinions. Xavier never caught a break, and if anyone deserved one, it was him. It was my brother."

Incorrect.

"Um, when I heard . . . I lost the only other person who could read my mind from the other side of a room. Do you know what it feels like to lose a brother? Anyone here? Because when I wake up in the morning, I don't have him to call. I mean, I try." He chokes on his words and pauses. "I try whenever I forget for a split second, and I get a voicemail over and over. Sometimes I want to tell him about some good news, and I can't. Instead, I get to watch the videos we made for social media over and over again. And every single time, I want to be that person again who has his brother next to him."

He looks around to the jury, all shaking their heads and holding back their obvious emotional responses. One girl in particular is tearing along with him. God, I hate blondes.

"I don't mean to go on like this. I don't. But . . . I—I hope for Xavier's sake it wasn't this relationship that killed him . . . Because having someone was the only thing he wanted, for real."

The silence sends an itch down my spine. Let's please get this show on the road before he loses his mind and spews more bullshit about what a great guy he was.

"Do you recognize the defendant?" Arguably nicely polished nails point in my direction.

"Yes, ma'am."

"Could you name the defendant?"

"Arlissa Benson."

"And how do you know the defendant?"

The mourning look on his face that paints false grief falls, and for a brief moment we lock eyes. "Uh, she used to be friends with my wife."

"Was? So that would be no longer, correct?"

Oh, fuck this.

"Correct."

"Right . . ." Mara takes a few steps back and ponders her next question.

"And who might your wife be?"

26

"Alejandra Garcia-Moore."

"And her stage name would be Aly, correct?"

"Yes."

"So, you would say you've been surrounded by public figures your entire life, including at this very moment?"

"Yes."

Evelyn stands, clearly as irritated by this as I am. "Please, the point."

Mara doesn't even look at her but instead straight to the judge. "I'm getting to my point soon, Your Honor."

"Please do."

"One last question, Mr. Moore, as I understand this hasn't been easy for you in the slightest. Given your experience with forming relationships and having a celebrity status, do you think the defendant only had an interest in using Xavier's name and wealth?"

Uh-oh.

Shut up.

Greyson's eyes meet mine once again, almost as if this wasn't on his question sheet. The answer to this one inquiry will redirect headlines for weeks—redirect the jury's opinion of me. My heart begins to beat out of my chest, but I can't let it be too obvious. The gravity of it all only sinks in briefly, but it's enough to bring my wall down for just a moment. Fear sneaks back in. The fear of losing control. It may be better to let go, but when the weight of the world is pressing down on my shoulders, what else do I do?

"Yes."

"Nothing further, Judge."

The destructive crack in my shield is so loud that I know I'm not the only one who hears it.

"Ms. Cyrus?"

Evelyn quickly stands, pressing her hands against her gray skirt. "Hello, Greyson." Her highlighted hair is straight today, unlike the other days where she put a heated curl to it. I try to focus on that instead of the sniffling coming from one of the jurors. Did she think he meant everything he said? How idiotic.

"Hello." He relaxes, oddly enough.

"How many conversations have you had with Arlissa in the five years that you've known her?"

He pauses for a moment, looking down as if he's counting on his fingers discreetly. "Maybe four times or so."

"So you'd say you don't know my client at all?"

He shrugs, the smug look on his face returning as if he didn't pull a Broadway-worthy tear factory out of his ass. "I wouldn't say that either."

"But everything you do know about her would be from someone else?"

"Correct."

That's my girl.

Chapter

FOUR

I'm home," I shout through the halls. It doesn't sound the same as it did in the condo. I wish I could go back there. I'd die fifty times over to live that life again. "Hello?"

"In here!" The voice chimes from the living room.

I swiftly remove my blazer and hang it up on the coatrack near the door, an eyesore of an object built from dark oak, but I guess it wins in the convenience department. I bend over, removing one heel at a time and leaving them against the wall. The thermostat is higher than I'd like. The sweat beads running down my back make that clear as day.

"What did you feed her today?" I shout, taking more steps down the gray hall before turning into the homely kitchen. It's hideous, simple, and borderline insulting.

"Same thing as always!"

"Okay, and what was that?" I call back before grabbing

a glass and turning on the faucet to run the water until I'm sure it's ice cold.

"Formula, duh. Ya know, the baby protein powder." Her voice is getting closer; Hope must be sleeping. I shut off the faucet and allow my water to settle in the glass before taking a sip.

"No one on earth calls it that but you," I comment before raising the glass to my lips and gently scratching my scalp.

Ellie appears through the archway, revealing herself like I left her. Her aesthetic is complete with messy brown tresses—perfect for running your hands through—and portrait tattoos that poke out of her My Chemical Romance crop top. She's skinnier now. How much weight can one person lose? I noticed it a few weeks ago, and now her ribs are in full view every time she inhales. The elasticity in her face is gone, skin clutching tightly onto a sharp jawline and strong cheekbones. She steps closer with concern washing over her features because we both know what I came back from. And thank God I came back.

"Was she good today?" I ask.

"Mm-hmm. Nothing too major. She took her first steps, said 'momma,' and I was like whoa, kid. I am not your mom." Green eyes light up as she tries to shine a little light on the subject.

I scoff. "You're insane."

"How was it?"

My body leans against the counter as I try to recall the events of the last ten hours. "I don't know yet. It hasn't really processed."

"That's a better answer than horrible," she whispers,

but my vision remains focused on the single needle constellation tattoo on her forearm.

I miss your tattoos. The detail, the shading, the bleeding whenever you got a new piece. They were expensive and well done—like you.

The pulsing in my head returns. I try not to squeeze my eyes shut, because when I do—I see it. I see a future that comes if I don't win this case. I see myself strapped down to a table, but I'm fighting it as hard as I can. The doctor asks, "Do you want to be a butterfly?" As if I'm a child. I'm doped up, not in control of my responses, and for some reason I nod. I tell him yes. Then it cuts to me in a room on my own. Except I can't move. My hands are glued to my waist, and I can't flex my fingers. There's a person on the other side of the glass, and they tell me that I'll be released when I can relax. I look down. I'm in a straitjacket. A white straitjacket with blue and violet stripes.

"Hello . . . Earth to Arlissa . . . Girl, did you hear me?" She's seated now, sipping on a Diet Coke that I didn't even see her retrieve.

"Yeah. Um. Yeah. I've just been having these weird dreams? Or . . . daydreams? I don't know. It comes with the migraines." I fan my hand down to signal to the woman not to worry.

"Uh . . . Okay? It's probably stress. I mean, you are going through literal hell right now. But I was just saying, I have to go to one of Nolan's games tonight. I'd stay but—"

"Yeah, no problem! I get it. Thanks for taking care of her again. I really appreciate it."

"Of course. I'm not leaving yet, though, so calm down. Don't get too excited." She pauses to take a few giant gulps out of her glass soda bottle. "Did you want to talk about those migraines? Thought I lost you for a second."

Tired hands pull out a chair from the dining table that we only have the space to keep in the kitchen. "Depends." The words drip out with maximum effort from my throat. "I didn't sleep last night, and I mean, I never do, but it's like it's getting worse. I don't know if it's Hope getting older and waking up or—I don't know. It could be stress like I said."

Or you're going fucking insane. Do you remember anything before the last few days?

Shut up.

"Yeah . . . That sounds like something a few painkillers can't fix. Try coke again." She chuckles, but I envy her. Ellie can still do her drugs without remorse. Ellie can go out into the world. She has movie premier invites in between making me feel as safe as possible. She's a friend I don't deserve. I'm more than aware of that. But the longer I talk to her, the more alone I feel.

She doesn't do it on purpose. I know that much. But she doesn't understand the weight that her words hold. Ellie has to go to a basketball game for her basketball player boyfriend. Ellie has to respond to an email about a product because Ellie is an influencer. Ellie still has her fucking life, and mine is gone in the wind. In the midst of all these actions and reactions, the butterfly effect does not work in my favor. How could something so small be the reason for such chaos? It all started when I met him. Or was it when I met her?

"I did some research on Marie Manning . . ." I blurt out in a desperate attempt to keep her attention.

I push one of the pillows to the side in order to make room for the both of us. Once she notices me, she sees all of me. Her head turns fully in my direction, and her big brown eyes accept the fact that she is safe. I've never felt that before, not as long as I can remember at least, and for that I envy her. I envy her because she has me, and I'll protect her until my dying breath. Her gaze is pure, casting a warm bright light over my entire body every time I join her space. I am capable of loving and receiving. And in this child's eyes, I see that as my truth. Every single time. But it only lasts as long as she's willing to look at me.

3945 Miller Road.

I didn't get much of a choice. Ellie loaned it to me. She told me she had a place she would run to when things got too hectic, a place I could call home until this all blew over. It's small, quaint, and the perfect place to quietly raise a baby. I was terrified of downgrading from my life of penthouses and central air. But when we got out of the car and what little belongings I still had were hauled out of the trunk—a rainbow appeared.

I whined about the rain the whole ride there as if there weren't worse things going on. But sometimes whining about trivial problems is easier than acknowledging being on trial for murder and hiding a pregnancy. The rainbow didn't show itself until I was standing pitifully in the sweatshirt that Alejandra managed to smuggle out of that condo for me. Back when she liked me, of course. I don't think she's ever understood what it's like to truly feel alone, and I guess that's what made me so easy to leave behind.

The colors decorated the sky and reminded me that everything that was once dull and sucky wouldn't feel that way forever. It was an arc without a foundation, a path without a set location. It was the rationale for me calling Ellie in the first place. The reason I realized that one day I'd return to the world he gave me. And ever since then, 3945 Miller Road became my safe haven.

"Now that you've eaten, I should . . . probably eat, myself." I smile and gently put Hope down and rise from my seat on the couch, vertebra by vertebra. Hope remains peaceful in her bundle of blankets, and for a brief second I forget the chaos that has become my entire existence. Sure, there are days where I can't believe she exists, but then I caress her skin, and it's a clear reminder. Her lips are pouty, and her eyelashes are thick and longer than mine ever were. She keeps herself in a bundled position and holds the pink blanket in between her neck and chin.

I quickly walk over to the kitchen, opening the fridge in hopes that I have some meal replacement shakes left. My heart rate increases even though I'm only a split second away from her. But anything could happen. She could fall off the couch or hit herself in the face. I scan the mostly vacant fridge for my shakes. Why aren't they right in the front? A phantom cry makes my heart jump—I stop and listen. Nothing. I move the carton of milk out of the way to reveal one of my plastic bottles. Thank God. Eager hands snatch it out of the fridge and slam the door so that I can rush back to my daughter.

"It's just us today," I whisper as I take a seat on the burgundy cushions. The muted TV plays *Saved by the Bell,* and I can't help but smirk. "This used to be Aly's favorite show. It would play on her TV when she didn't have cable, and even though it seemed stupid and way too old to watch, she made me watch it." I giggle, and Hope doesn't even look at me. But it's nice to say these things out loud. I untwist the cap from the bottle and allow the thick cold liquid to travel down my throat. "I hope you can meet her one day."

Hope coos casually as if she's contributing to the conversation. "I wonder what Alejandra would do . . . if she was in this situation, I mean." I look down at the baby and run my fingers through her already thick hair. "Do you know? Well, I'll make an assumption. If Alejandra was talking to me, she'd probably swat me on the head and tell me to get up and stop hiding. She'd totally tell me to go shout to whoever will listen about how bad I'm being screwed. Cause a racket. Burn them all alive. And she'd get what she wants. I guess I gotta channel my inner Alejandra, right?"

My smile feels genuine for the first time in a long time. It feels fresh, as if I'm smiling at something new. Like a child who just had their first fire-roasted s'more prepared by their father. I miss my father. I miss my life.

"I miss her . . ."

I shake my head in a desperate attempt to snap out of it and place the barely touched shake onto the coffee table. Hope is paying me no mind and is instead fascinated by open space.

Out of sight, out of mind.

"I'll be right back," I say and quickly run to the back room where my cell phone is hidden. I check it once a day, usually around the same time in case Evelyn or Madison need to get ahold of me for some sort of fire drill. I open the bedside dresser drawer and pull out the device that used to be attached to my hand. It glows as it turns on while I walk back to where Hope is. Still peaceful, as if she's giving me the time I need to do some snooping.

I want to know. I know it'll be bad to know, but I do. Did Aly see my outburst? Is there a clue left for me that tells me she misses me too?

My body sinks onto the hardwood flooring, and my back rests against the sofa. Hope's feet brush against the nape of my neck a few times, but I don't mind it. Notifications flood the top of the screen, most being from Ellie hoping that I'm not reeling over our argument. I'm not. But I don't have the energy to deal with that right now. Chipped fingernails click on the internet app and go straight to the search button. Aly.

> Q   Aly | Official Site.

> Q   Aly- Another Love Song (Official Video)

> Q   Aly- For Us (Live)

Boring. Boring. Boring. News.

> Q   Aly Looks Stunning with New Blunt Bangs
>   and Long Wavy Hair

> Q   Aly Confirms She Is "Working on My Album"

> Q   Inside Aly and Greyson's SNL After-party

> Q   Greyson and Xavier's Complicated Timeline

Oh? I click the link, scrolling past photos that make my heart turn and twist in a million different directions. My vision drops to a related article, one that I check the date a million times first before believing it. Posted today. My heart skips a few beats, panging and gnawing at my chest like it wants to jump out.

> 🔍 Vanessa Carter Mourns Hidden
> Relationship with Xavier Amari

What fucking relationship? I click to see a woman with more silicone in her body than I have in my house. It's nicely done. I can't knock that. Her lip fillers are also pretty nice, along with all the Botox in her face. Her black hair is accompanied by what I can only imagine are tape-ins. The article goes into detail about things I don't even have the mental clarity to read right now. My eyes dart to the images that I hope are a joke or they're old. Who the hell is she?

It is Xavier in those photos. That much is obvious. One with his arm wrapped around her in a hotel room mirror. Another with him just getting out of the shower, smiling ear to ear with a towel wrapped around his waist. I keep scrolling to a video—they're at dinner. He's mouthing I love you. But the person on the other end of the camera isn't me—it's her.

I check the tattoos on his body, the length of his hair, and the clothes on his back. It all points to a time that hits too close to home. Everything detailed on him dates these images to *our* last year. The late nights, the random trips, the overworking, the boredom when I spoke, and the bare minimum tolerance of my very existence. The tiny mannerisms that were cold enough to drive me to text Christian when he wouldn't come home. But the dogs and fiery moments that reminded me that he loved me. I miss my dogs. Wow. It was all because he cheated. Did I know? No, I couldn't have.

Tears rush down my cheeks while my brain scrambles to fit the puzzle pieces together. Hope squirms behind me like she knows what I'm feeling, like she can sense it from me. The throbbing in my head appears and then intensifies within seconds, like it did on the night he banged my head against the brick. He was so nonchalant when he took me back, like he didn't care one bit. Did I know?

You knew.

Were you just waiting for me to give up but instead I beat you to the punch?

Probable.

You broke me into shattered glass and watched me bleed more times than I can count. You cheated. You fucking cheated. Did I know when you were arguing with Savannah and I hid in the hall because I couldn't face seeing the two of you standing near each other in person? When did I know? My heart sinks to the pit of my stomach as I shakily stand from the floor. The two legs that carry me forward are now numb. Tears continue to stream down my cheeks and onto my cotton shirt.

Hope has started crying. But I can't bring myself to turn around.

You cut at my velvet skin, and I still crawled back begging for your affections. You craved victory no matter how petty the situation, and found comfort in knowing you'll always be right. You cheated. Did you know my mind was elsewhere and wanted to get me back first? Or did you not give enough of a shit about me to resist the temptations that a woman named Vanessa carried? You told me let's have a baby! Even after losing our first! There are no excuses here. You were always the problem.

And now I've lost everything.

I stand in front of the mirror in the bathroom where if I take one step forward, I bump into the sink. And if I take one step to the left, I fall into the tub. The mirror hasn't been cleaned for weeks, so I run the water and wipe it a few times with my wrist. Fuck you, at least my veins are still intact. Can you say the same?

I aggressively pull at my cheeks to wipe the salty liquid away. I pull and tug until my skin stings and turns a bright red. Hope's screaming from the living room only escalates, but I'm screaming right with her. I'm screaming until my lungs burn. God, I wish she'd shut up and let me have this. I wish everyone would just let me have this.

My breath quickens, and the blood in my body feels like it's boiling. There were a few years where I never thought it'd get this low. I was on award show stages in my Cinderella ball gown; I had peaked. My vision drops to the mascara tube on the sink, I grab it and belligerently pop it open. My hands are shaking as I try desperately to apply some of the makeup onto my eyelashes. The substance gets on my eyelids, and it's so old now that it clumps every so often on the few lashes it's able to dress. My tears cause the wet mascara to fall down my cheeks. I try to wipe it but just end up getting black ink smudged all over my hands and face.

"I'm—I'm your host, Arlissa Benson." I stare at myself in the mirror and smile. Superstars always smile. "And it is so amazing to be here with you guys. Can we give it up for everyone in the building tonight?" Hope screams in response. It sounds like she's losing her voice now. I grip tightly onto the tube of makeup that is now acting as my mic. I imagine myself in that blue dress—it still fits perfectly. Xavier's in the crowd, and so is Aly. They're cheering me on. I'm not just looking at seats filled with strangers but also friends. "W-we have so many am-amazing presenters and performers tonight and I-I-I loved watching them rehearse." Smile bigger. "Y'all do not understand what they have in store for you." I stare blankly into the reflection and force out a casual laugh, just like I would if I had another chance to do this again. I imagine the crowd roaring just like they had before. Everyone is cheering and clapping for me. Not for him or Vanessa Carter, who was probably going to be my replacement. Me. "Th-thank you." Hope quiets down, she must have given up on trying to get my attention by now. "Thank you. And now for the rest of the show."

Chapter
SIX

They always say the first day is the hardest, but I'm willing to challenge that as the truth. It's the second and every day after that until the end. But of course, you end up in those unlucky situations that make you wonder if anything really ever ends. Life, court dates, doctor's appointments. They all come to a time-stamped end, but the remnants from them lingers forever. Whether it be emotional trauma or eternal joy, I've grown to believe that nothing truly ends.

Evelyn choosing to wear her hair in a bun today could easily become a staple for minority lawyers for years to come. She could say the right sentence, and people will run and get quote tattoos. Or we could lose, and she'd lose all her credibility. Who knows?

I know this is a high-profile case. Madison is sure to remind me every time we walk into the courthouse. The fact that I chose to wear cherry-red lipstick on day two of court could easily become something just as recognizable as Marilyn Monroe in that white dress. A Halloween costume for the college girls. It all depends on what happens today.

And that is why nothing ever ends, because the constant suspense of someone else being able to shift your world with their actions is fucking terrifying. Control. Whether you believe you ever wanted it or not, Arlissa, you need it. And maybe you need it just as bad as I did. It's okay to admit that.

"What happened just after three in the morning on July 15, 2020, was a tragedy. That night, Arlissa Benson woke up to her boyfriend"—Evelyn pauses, gulping so visibly hard you would think she dated him too—"who she loved more than anything in the world."

Did you, though?

Why are you even here?

Why haven't you gotten rid of me? Too desperate for something to comfort you when those nightmares happen?

The wind feels as if it's been knocked out of my lungs because I know he's only asking that question out of spite.

Two years with Ms. Normal. There is no way in hell I loved you. I had it all. I had Savannah. I had the name. I had the friends. I had the money. And that's why I was cheating. I know you want to ask about her. Doesn't mean I'm going to answer. You see, that's where you've been missing it. That's where you've been confused and fucking stupid, shortstack. It always comes back to control. I didn't live and die with the dire need to control you. Or, hell, anyone for that matter. No one, including you, was ever that special. I wanted to have my fun and get the hell out. You should have thanked me.

Then he stops.

"Good morning, Arlissa. How are you feeling today?" Another voice creeps into my mind. The deep and cautious sounds of a stranger. I can't put a face to the voice, but it's familiar.

And then another. This one is softer, more concerned than the first. "She hasn't been responding to the medicine." It comes through clearly while everything else sounds like I've turned the dial to the wrong radio station. In and out, between this courtroom and—where else?

My eyes slowly drift from my folded hands on this wooden table to anything that has the power to stop the ringing in my ears. In the top right corner of the courtroom, a figure appears as if it belongs. Suit and tie, slicked-back dark hair that had freshly been cut, and scruff that only appeared when he didn't have the time to shave it. His tan skin is paler now, replicating a ghostly look that even I couldn't visualize on my own. Because I'm not; because he's here.

Xavier takes a few steps toward me, removing the breath from my lungs every time his suede shoes hit the polished brown floors.

Don't cry. Don't change your breathing. Maintain control. He looks around the courtroom as if he's the one on trial, analyzing everyone's body language with his sharp stare like the world is his stage and he's just waiting to captivate them. *Look.* He points to the three people seated diagonally from me. *Slowly. Don't make it too obvious that you're staring; you were always bad at that.* I use my curly bangs to hide my pupils slowly peering off behind me, turning my head molecule by molecule.

Channel 3 is seated right there. The kid with the glasses who looks like this is his first day on the job. Not too sure how they cleared that. Okay, look a bit more. STOP! You don't want to look like you're trying. They're recording you. See the dude holding the camera with bagel crumbs in his beard? You never look at him, you watch out for him, and you only give yourself a moment to breathe when he's not looking. But unfortunately for you, he'll always be looking.

"And when she saw him, drenched in blood, it didn't make sense at the time, and it doesn't make sense today." Another pause. The jury is in the palm of her hand with gawking stares and slouching stances. "And it will never make sense because it is insanity."

He takes Evelyn's seat next to me, replicating my sitting style almost perfectly, down to the crossed legs. *Aw shit, didn't you guys agree not to do that?*

"You are going to hear a lot of evidence in this case. You will hear it in the form of witness testimony. You will hear from law enforcement, mental health professionals using complicated terms that you may not understand. There's going to be a lot of information, some of which you may also not understand. Just keep in mind what you're here for. And thank you so much for returning, we all appreciate it because we know this is a lot to both hear about and see."

You see what she's doing? She's telling them—

I kick myself into gear, drowning him out like I had to do to Samantha all those years. He stops talking, the ringing in my ears stops, and I feel fully present again. Samantha was never right here with me, though. She always came across like a trick of the mind and never something that if I reached out far enough I could touch. I wonder if I could . . .

Snap out of it. Stay in character.

I straighten my back and listen, listen for any sign that I'm not losing my fucking mind. "This case didn't start in July of 2020. Unfortunately, Ms. Benson has struggled with the limelight, ups and downs, and mental illness for years before this event occurred. At the age of seven, she witnessed the brutal murder of her older sister and had to be seen by many mental health professionals following the incident."

My skin starts to boil as I get a taste of how finite of a resource self-control is. I swallowed my anger when it was a bomb, and now it seems like someone has taken the pin out. When a bomb explodes, fire-red flames cover its surroundings, and I have been trying so hard to stop from burning everything to ash. But this? This is unacceptable.

"Unfortunately for Ms. Benson, mental health was never the focus of the adults in her life. You will hear that from seven years old to about eighteen years old, she had a shell that she couldn't quite manage to break out of. A shell that was made of fear and a result of neglect. She received counseling, she was receiving medications, but oddly enough no one around her can tell you how many of these counseling sessions occurred. So, unfortunately, at about age ten, getting the child help was no longer a priority."

My body continues to shake as my mind focuses on the biggest question—how? How does she know things I had conveniently left out of every version of my life that I've told?

"Mom was drinking more than she should have been, and Dad had to go upstate to take care of some business, so Arlissa's growth became the responsibility of whatever friends she met along the way—one of which you'll be hearing from."

Oh! There it is. Aly's coming! Xavier has a big grin on his face, focused on everyone else and not even turning to look at me. Does he not miss me? Who knows how long we'll have.

"You'll hear that there was a huge breakup between the pair, and from the witnesses it would have been their worst and final. Someone that she had depended on; she had to go to the hospital to treat the injuries that he gave her. You'll hear from the medical professionals what that could do to someone's mental state. This case will never make rational sense because it is indeed insanity."

No it's fucking not.

I mean, it might be.

Evelyn continues to pace around the room like she's on fire, and arguably she is. The jury is already drawing their conclusions, and I can see it all from their intrigued facial expressions. Each and every one of them is stuck on her like a dog and she's got peanut butter on her fingers.

"The first responders will tell you she wasn't making sense. She was rambling. And why wouldn't she be? Nobody, and I mean nobody, is disputing that what happened that night is tragic. But if you feel that your heart strings are being intentionally tugged on, pay attention to that. We have to focus on the evidence."

Chapter
SEVEN

*I*t's amazing how ignorant people can be when they want to be. I mean it is bliss, and we tend to choose bliss at our earliest convenience. Here's an example: Evelyn choosing to adjust the cuffs on her white cotton suit and ignoring the tears welling up in my eyes. Insanity. We talked about it; we said we wouldn't do it.

I remember being too scared to speak up. No matter how many showers I took, I could still see the bloodstains under my fingernails and on my legs. No matter how many times I changed clothes, I still felt as exposed as I was in that white satin nightgown. My eyes remained a constant bright red for weeks after. People looked at me like I was a monster, even the ones who felt bad for me. There was nothing conventional about how I was coping, the words I was saying, or the thoughts I was thinking.

That version of me was weak and pitiful. There was a point, when the clocks went back and the wind gained in aggression, that I changed. The sun's warmth wasn't enough to protect me from the stone-cold truth that those December days provided. Orange rays didn't allow me to bask in it anymore while it made its slow departure like it attempted to on those July mornings and September evenings. The sun stopped setting slowly but rather like it was in a rush. A rush to get back home, like I was.

And for an entire season I stopped hearing him. It was dead silence even though every man in California looked like him from a distance. During the winter I was able to look past that. When the cold came out, I stopped feeling him in the warmth. I always knew the sun was a star, but I never experienced it firsthand before. Not until he was no longer there. That was when I understood everything he was talking about, and in the dead of winter I was reborn. That was when I finally spoke up for myself.

Evelyn had been meeting with me to ensure that everything was okay and that I hadn't ripped open my veins. Thanks to Alejandra, I was out on bail, and that was the last good deed she did until she ultimately bailed herself. After visit number six, Evelyn finally felt like it was time to talk strategy. I remember sitting there, shivering under a Snuggie and sweatpants. It felt like I was already on trial.

"I think we should go with the insanity plea. I went through the discovery provided, and there's enough evidence to get you convicted, and it's the best play we have. I'm sorry that I can't sugarcoat this for you."

I stared blankly at the coffeepot behind her, hoping that what I heard wasn't true. The brown liquid filled the glass with urgency, knowing exactly what action it was to perform whenever it was turned on. I was never a huge coffee drinker, not until I depended on the brewer to give my day-to-day life some structure. It helped with no longer self-medicating my anxious nights. But it kept me up. This was one of those mornings after a horrifying sleepless night.

"No."

"Excuse me?"

"No. Insanity is basically saying I did it, and I didn't do it."

I remember how Evelyn's normally bronzed features went pale, completely flustered by the words that were leaving my lips. "It's not about the truth. It's about getting you the best possible outcome."

"That's bullshit. Find something else."

She never spoke about the approach again. Yet here we are.

"I'd like to bring to the stand first responder, Officer Kevin Solis."

Evelyn takes her seat next to me again, allowing the prosecutor to make her way back to center stage. As she's getting her papers in order, a hefty man walks onto the podium. His entire appearance comes off as someone who just rolled off of a Ringling Bros. tour bus. However, he's dressed in a cop uniform where the sleeves are too short and the pants are too tight. In fact, if I squint just a bit more, I can see a stain right above the crotch. Who would come to court like that?

He doesn't sit immediately, stopping to put his right hand up and mumble the same vow that everyone is required to say but no one is fully committed to following.

The fairly older security guard speaks, directing the witness over to his seat. "Now, sir, if you would have a seat in the burgundy chair. Make sure you speak in a loud and clear voice for the recordings. Thank you."

Officer Solis clears his throat above the microphone, the sound rumbling through the courtroom like a thunderstorm. There's a smirk on his face. One I'd mistake as innocent if I didn't know any better. Nothing about him is familiar. He turns to the jury and introduces himself as if this is a class presentation and not a murder trial.

Mara looks up at the officer and smiles slightly. "What is your occupation?"

"I am a police officer for the Los Angeles Police Department."

"How long have you been on the force?"

"Eleven years."

Sure looks like it. But donuts and paperwork had to be the bulk of it.

"Was all of that with the Los Angeles Police Department?"

Officer Solis pushes his glasses up and takes a moment to answer. "Yes."

I calmly scan the colorless room in hopes of a beacon of light that can save me from the heaviness in my heart. Hope. I know she should be the reason I swallow my pride and find something to trust in Evelyn again. But instead I'm just looking for Xavier.

"What is your current assignment today?"

I'm looking for him in the police officer that I don't recognize. I'm looking for him in the bare tan walls surrounding us.

"I am currently a field training officer."

"And what was your assignment on July 15, 2020?" The one-year anniversary was just a few weeks ago.

"I was a field training officer."

"And while doing this job, you were on patrol. Is that correct?"

"It is."

Look at how he keeps looking at her for answers. I jump in my seat a bit, not expecting the voice to appear behind me, but just like clockwork he appears. My eyes first drop to my sea-green blazer, hoping to focus on that in order to buy me enough time to rebuild my poker face. *Mara asks the questions, but our buddy Solis over here allows himself a brief second before looking up and getting some kind of visual confirmation. Pay attention. Pay attention to the fact that you have never seen this man before, Arlissa.*

"And what are you expected to do as a patrol officer?"

"Uh, typically reply to 911 calls, as well as traffic stops and other activities regarding reported incidents."

"And do you remember the evening going into the early hours of the night on July 15, 2020?"

Another pause, but he nods this time, making direct eye contact with the jury. Tell me you're noticing this shit.

I am.

"I do."

"And how did the night of July 15, 2020, go for you, Officer Solis?"

He twirls his chair nervously, and I can only assume the contents of his lower body are spilling out from the sides of that seat. The single cushion crying for help, kind of how I have been since the fifteenth of July. "It went well, was quiet at first, not much going on at all. Not until the call at least."

"Can you describe what happened around three in the morning on July 15, 2020?"

"I was actually about to go on my meal break."

"And do you usually have your meal break around Wilshire Boulevard?"

"No, I just chose to drive in that direction that night. The plan was to park, unpack the lunch my wife made for me, and hope to get an uninterrupted hour."

"And what were you driving?"

"A marked police cruiser. A Crown Victoria, I believe. Number 4832."

Why doesn't he know that for sure? Arlissa, come on.

No.

Come on!

His voice roars in my ears, causing a rattling against my eardrums that makes me wince. I can feel Evelyn's eyes peer in my direction, but if I look at her, I'll snap.

If you don't do anything right now, you should at least keep your cool.

I know.

"What were you wearing?"

Solis smirks, but Mara doesn't find it funny. Her shoulders hike up, and she straightens her stance as much as possible.

"I was wearing our LAPD uniform."

"Just after three in the morning, did you receive a dispatch call?"

"I did."

"Could you please tell me what happened?"

"In short, there was a disturbance at one of the condos right up the street from me. They said someone was hurt and there was a lot of blood as well as screaming and arguing. Given the address, I estimated that I was the closest to the condominiums, so I headed there as fast as possible."

"What happened after that?" Mara's voice is breathy and low, but somehow every word is echoing in my head clear as day. In Xavier's voice.

"I was able to get into the lobby of the apartment building. I had already called for backup at this point, and by the time I got upstairs, the front door was already ajar."

"May I stop you there? Was the door fully open?"

"No. Only slightly. About enough to fit my foot through."

No. No. We would never leave the door open. Especially not that night. Especially not Xavier. I sit up, feeling the sweat beads trickle down my back, the blouse's fabric sticking to my skin.

"Do you have any idea why the door was open?"

"No, we never got the answer to that question."

Yes, because it was never open. Laughter brings my attention to the judge's bench. Xavier sits there with his legs crossed, same suit but in a coral color this time. *That doesn't even sound logical. Was there a fight? Shit!* He kicks his feet up, slapping his large hand on his knee. *Did we fight?*

My head begins to pound, creating the kind of headache that has the ability to stop all the traffic in my brain. *Focus on me!* it screams, waving its big red stop sign. Usually I'd find a place to rest—a place to hide. But in this courtroom, there isn't a corner to ride out the storm in or a speck of dust to hide under. The judge shoots a look of concern in my direction, like she's noticing the chaos rummaging between my temples.

"And what happened after that?"

"I slowly entered the home. At that point I turned on my flashlight and unholstered my weapon. The entire condominium was silent. I could only hear my own footsteps."

"What kind of weapon?"

"My gun."

"At what point did you call out?"

"I didn't. I wasn't too positive about the circumstances or who or what I was walking into, so I didn't say anything."

"Until when?"

"Until I saw the bedroom."

"And what did you see when you saw the bedroom?"

"At first, nothing. There was a limited amount of visibility due to it being pitch black in the home. But from my flashlight and the light in the window, I saw a couple sleeping in bed."

"Was this the point where your backup had arrived?"

"Yes."

"And were you instructed to wait for them to get upstairs?"

"Yes. They had a better sense of who lived in the building by then and knew that the occupants of that particular condominium were Arlissa Benson and Xavier Amari."

"At this point, had you noticed that Xavier Amari was deceased?"

"No."

"And how far apart were they from each other?"

"Not far at all. If I hadn't gotten the call, I would have thought I was walking in on a couple who were peacefully sleeping together. He had his arm around her, and she had her arm over him."

"What side was she on? Left side, right side?"

"The left side, by the window. He was closer to the in-room bathroom."

"Is the woman you saw in the bed in this courtroom?"

"Yes."

"Can you point to her?"

"Yes."

I don't look up to see if he's pointed at me, but by the fiery stinging on my left side I know he has.

"Your backup shows up, you enter the room, and then what?"

"When we were all able to move in on the scene, all of our flashlights were able to see the blood on not only her gown but the sheets. We also were able to see the lacerations across his wrists. As soon as Ms. Benson saw the lights, she jumped up."

"And did you arrest her then?"

"We did. She had blood on her hands and on her nightgown."

"And did anything happen when you arrested her?"

"She started screaming that she had done it. Over and over again."

And you can't even get up and let the whole world know that that doesn't look anything like your arresting officer. Oh, and the FBI tag. What about that? Face it, Arlissa. You're crazy.

Chapter

EIGHT

45. 50. 62.

My foot presses hard on the gas, fully in control of where the vehicle goes next. The trees are changing from distinct figures on my right side to colorless images that I no longer recognize. My speedometer glows in the moonlight, no longer matching the numbers on the black-and-white sign posted on the highway. I grip the wheel until my nails dig into the bottom of my palms and hold them there. I press until blood is drawn, because whether this car crashes or I get my DNA on the wheel, at least someone will know I was here.

65. 70. 74.

So I step on it. The engine hums, and the silver beams marking the space between the road and the forest seem to look more like a challenge than a caution. I step on it, because at the very least someone will finally take the time to listen to what I have to say. I step on the gas, and I don't let it go, because going this fast is the only strength I know. I step on the pedal because when everything is a blur, I can't be dragged into mourning by a brain I'm supposed to trust. Maybe if I go fast enough, the red paint will peel off and I won't have another physical reminder of a birthday I won't be able to go back to. The hill—it's right off this exit.

77. 83. 92.

If hitting one hundred is the only accomplishment I know before going to prison, then so fucking be it. What was the point of it all? Getting sober? Having a child with no real father figure in sight? Loving someone who had always been a cheater? Looking into the mirror and hating what stared back at me with every fiber of my being? What was the point of cutting my hair in the bathroom and screaming until my lungs gave out? One hand releases the wheel, clicking the red seat belt button and watching it retract before the top of the hill comes into full view. I used to hike here. I used to watch the sunset here. And now, would it be so bad to crash my car here? Allow life to truly come full circle?

92. 96. 99.

The engine screams like a child that wants desperately to get out of the trunk. I let it. I let it get as loud as it needs to and disrupt whomever it pleases, because no one is ever considerate of me. No one asks me how I'm doing. No one asks me what goes on in my head, and no one ever has. Being here in this driver's seat—where I control the outcome. Well, it feels like flying. The number of trees increases. I know that much because I've been here before, but in reality everything around me looks like a contemporary painting. Distorted, blurred, color splashed against canvas, and maybe if I—

100.

The color bombs clear up. Only because I'm now being greeted with a clear opening by the moonlight. I keep my hands on the wheel. Just a few more feet and this car will go completely off the cliff. I can just shut my eyes. I can forget about all of it. But I will never be forgotten about. My actions will be picked apart by the media when I'm gone. They'll say that I was whomever fits their narrative best. Or—

"Hey! Slow down!" a woman screams from the top of the hill.

I'm getting closer to her every moment. I ease on the brake. Why isn't she moving out of the way? I stomp on the brake now and whip both arms to the left.

My body jerks forward and almost launches itself out of the seat, but it doesn't. My eyes are forced shut, but the car—the car is stopped. Thick liquid flows past my eyebrows. I want to touch it, but I can't. One moment the edge of the cliff is there, open and welcoming; the next, I can't open my eyes because I have no idea what I'll be opening them to. Did I brake in time? Is it over? Did I hit her?

I feel as though I'm looking without seeing, trying to get a sense of every limb and body part before I'm tasked with the job of coming to terms with the visual trauma that is realizing what I've done. A mental scan of my body alerts me of one thing in particular, my head. The one thing I can't trust is the first thing I check on when I've put it in danger.

I hope, at the very minimum, I don't survive whatever this is. I hope it ends here. I hope Hope finds a way to live a life where she can go to the park with her mother and not live in fear of paparazzi. I hope she never grows up knowing that she was an at-home birth because the fear of letting the whole world know something that I refuse to prove is too much. And I am so grateful she made it here safe and sound. She deserves the best, and I am not that. Xavier knew. Samantha knew. Aly knew. And that is why everyone I have ever known has never stayed long enough to watch the end credits of my movie with me. I'm sitting in this seat, doing this alone. The way it was always intended to be.

"Hey! Over here. No. Yes. Well! She was speeding, but I think she's okay. Oh God, her head."

"What do we do?"

"Put her in your car!"

NINE

*W*hat would normally be a soft yellow glow from my bedroom light is replaced by a harsh white illumination that drags me away from the world of dreams to a grim reality. Have I been asleep? Did I sleep this long without any issues? Where's Hope? Where am I?

The beeping of the machines that are latching onto me is steady. I'm steady.

You know, I was doing some reading. Without my eyes open, I can see him in high definition. *What do you think a ghost is, Arlissa? Other than what you were trying to become, of course.* He stands there in the empty dark space my brain has created for him. This time Xavier's dressed in a pair of black scrubs with a blue coat thrown over it. *A ghost is just unfinished business. Salman . . . Salman something said that! My point is, what's a person with unfinished business if they're not a ghost? A figment of your imagination, that's what. Which is what I am, what you are. Which means you and I will always be the same.*

No. I loved you, and you didn't love anyone but yourself.

He sighs, his non-slip shoes causing an echo with every step he takes. *People do this thing where they remove their villains from reality. They curate them into these beings capable of such great evil. They do this in order to no longer see themselves in it. Because God forbid you like the same music as Ted Bundy. Why would someone search up what music he listened to on weekends? They don't. They don't because they don't want to see themselves in someone like Ted Bundy, Richard Ramirez, Jack the Ripper, John Wayne Gacy. I could go on and on and on. But the main point is, you don't want to see yourself in me. So you tell yourself we're different, but we're exactly alike.*

My eyes shoot open like my name is Raven and I just had a vision. Suddenly, my feet are clammy and the sheets have melted onto my skin. My pulse accelerates, and nothing around me feels real anymore. Light blue walls that are supposed to instill a sense of calm in me only quicken my breathing. But then they switch to gray, then back to blue. I blink a few more times; there's a large doctor standing in front of my bed—then there isn't. The room changes with every blink from my nightmares to an empty hospital room. I shake my head vigorously, begging the images to go away.

"Hey . . . Hey. You're all right."

I turn to the voice, furrowing my brows in an attempt to understand why a random blond woman is in my room.

She smiles reassuringly. "You look confused. I'm Nina. I'm, uh . . . the one you almost hit with your car.

My brother drove you here. You kind of passed out. He thought you'd be more comfortable if you saw me first instead of him. He's right out there." She points to the shut door with a small window placed in the middle that shows me nothing but more blue paint. "Anyway! I'm rambling . . . You didn't have an ID on you, but I just wanted to make sure you were okay and ask if you had any family we could call?"

"Um . . ."

"You're fine. Nothing a doctor can't fix. Not sure how, really. You were like one inch away from flying through your windshield. Didn't, though. You must have some super dope guardian angels."

An empty laugh forces its way out of my mouth. "Yeah, I must."

"I'm sorry." She stands while her bitten-down finger-tips pull at the hem of her Pink Floyd tank top nervously. "I know we don't know each other, and my mouth runs a mile a minute. I'm just glad you're okay . . . I was minding my business and then vroom! This car comes out of nowhere." Her tone slows, forest-green pupils filled with sorrow, and suddenly I wish I knew what she was looking at. Is there a huge gash across my face? Is my hair matted from excess blood coming from a head wound? Nothing feels broken. I don't have any casts on.

"You're fine . . . um."

Before I can get any of my thoughts together, there's a faint knock at the door. Without any verbal approval, the door creaks open and reveals a hand covered in tattoos first. Then an arm decorated in colors and images only to be cut off by a short-sleeved T-shirt. A single black-and-white Jordan sneaker follows shortly after, and before I know it, the face of someone else I've never seen before is there. He nods at me, then focuses completely on the woman.

"Yo, Nina."

She sighs before pivoting to face him. "Hm?"

"We should get out of here now," he whispers and then turns his attention to me. "Hey, miss. Glad you're okay. But your mom is here to see you."

I frown, and my brows draw together. "Huh?"

He shrugs, and the frown on his face screams, *Don't ask me!*

"Well, alrighty then! I left my phone number and Nico's if you need anyone to call. I know he looks scary, you know, with the face tattoos and all. But I promise he's not."

He rolls his eyes. "Come on, give the girl some space."

"Okay, okay! Like I said, it's right there. We're both really glad you're okay." She grabs her purse out of the plastic chair and briefly stops to tie her Doc Martens boot. Once everything is where it should be, she uses her pointer finger to push her bangs out of her eyes. "All right. Well. Bye."

"Hey," I call out before the two strangers make their grand escape. "Thanks."

"Welcome."

"You are very welcome."

Once the door quietly shuts, I have a moment to myself. I take note of the fact that my headache has subsided and so has my blurry vision. I turn my head to the right, glancing at the scribbled-on notepad that she left there. Her number and her brother's number just like she said. And for some odd reason their emails too. I rip the paper off of the pad, noticing the scratches that look like they've been tended to already on my knuckles. No dried blood, just bare and red to make sure I know they're new. Black pupils stare at them as all the tension slowly leaves my body. *Snap out of it.* I quickly fold the paper for reasons I'm not too sure of and slip it under my pillow.

Suddenly, the door handle jiggles, and without any warning a woman with sunglasses and a scarf wrapped around her head enters. She doesn't look at me, but instead efficiently locks the door. I roll my eyes as the tension builds up throughout my entire being all over again. I knew it. If nothing else would get her attention, this surely would.

"You told them you were my mom?" I scoff as I watch her unravel herself like it's not the peak of summer.

"What? Is it not that believable?" Her country accent is less inviting these days, more threatening than anything else.

I cross my arms over my chest the best I can without wincing from the soreness. "Okay then."

Once she's done undressing, Amy is back to being the woman I remember. A classic red lip complemented by blond pin curls that would help you pick her out from any crowd. Red-bottom heels make their way over to me—but she refuses to sit down. "I covered this disastrous situation up for you."

"Right. For me."

"Oh no, don't thank me. You're only on trial for murdering my only son."

I purse my lips in reaction to her bold statement. Amy doesn't care. Amy sits there with her Birkin bags and YSL lipstick and revels in the sweet reminder that she has a billion dollars behind her. Amy can't be the face of chaos. I could set the Hollywood sign on fire, and she'd shuffle out

71

a small fraction to frame it on the heroin-addicted Twitch streamer down the street. Amy has a billion dollars stuffed into her tear ducts. So the first thing she did when her son died was use some of that cushion to shut me up. And it worked.

"I don't get why it's taking them so long to figure out that I didn't do anything. And you don't—you don't even answer the phone anymore."

Her attention drops to her cellular device, which results in a deadly silence lurking over the room. "Oh. You've been calling?"

"This is kind of important, Amy."

Suddenly, ruby-red fingernails grip onto my arm, only increasing the tenderness in my skin. It stings, but I swallow it. I've become used to swallowing the pinches, the throbs, the anguish, and the tearing. "You don't tell me what's important."

I snatch my arm away as far as I can while feeling glued to this bed. "No, I do. Because whether you admit it or not, you need me just as much as I need you."

The older woman steps back and scoffs. "Is that so?"

"You don't care whether I sink or swim, and I know that. I'm not a fucking idiot. But you care about his reputation, and I have a sneaky feeling that you and your fancy lawyer don't know how to get me out of this shit without admitting that he slit his veins willingly."

"You don't know how wrong you are, darling. Now get up. I'm taking you home."

"No." Hope. She can't know about Hope.

"What do you mean no?"

Quickly, Arlissa. Make her not want to be near you another second. "I said no."

"Get your stuff and come on, girl." Amy swipes my thigh before heading to the door.

"I haven't even been discharged."

"You are now."

"You don't get to do this." *For Hope. She can't know where you live, for her. You don't know much, but you know that much, right?* "You don't get to ignore me and then tell me what to do again. Where has listening to you got me?"

"It got you out of jail and with the top lawyer in the state."

Push her. My breath quickens as my mouth begins to feel like it's stuffed with a thousand balls of cotton. "You didn't deserve him, you know. Not after what you did to him."

Her defenses rise by the way she shields her chest with her arms and closes her hands into fists. "I raised a good boy. An honest boy. A boy who loved his momma. All the love in the world couldn't help that wretched soul of yours. You don't get to blame your corruption on me."

My voice begins to shake with every moment that I'm tasked with the responsibility of refraining from wiping that smug smile off of her face. "Face it, Amy. He didn't want to be around you just as bad as he didn't want to be around me. I have woken up every single day since then realizing that he felt like death was a better solution than answering another one of *our* calls. It is time that you wipe off the mask that you walk around in. The one where you don't answer the phone calls of the people you swore you'd help. The one where you won't publicly state that I didn't do a damn thing and you know that. The one where you own up to letting your husband beat on your only dead son."

She clenches her jaw but remains composed—somehow. "I was in pain, and I have every right to not pick up the phone when the person who drove my son over the edge is staring me in the face begging for a hand to hold."

"What about my pain?" I shout, tears flying across the room as adrenaline shoots me into a seated position. "What about his?" It comes out as a whimper while emotions show themselves as cascades down my cheeks.

She swallows hard but only calmly collects her sunglasses and begins wrapping her scarf around her head. Once, twice, three times until the blond locks are completely concealed. Makes sense, considering she's only comfortable when being hidden behind anything—or anyone. The woman keeps her purse at belly button level before allowing her chest to expand and compress within the same five second span. "Remember who pays for your freedom, Arlissa Benson."

Chapter

TEN

I rub the bandage across my head until the wound is irritated—yay, I can still feel things. A light hum comes from the neighbor's lawn mower to the right of me. I've never waved to him before, and today won't be the day. Cement-filled footsteps walk lazily up the driveway. I peer to my right. The security I personally hired is parked at his post across the street. My eyes are half-open, but as I make my way around the bushes and trees, the front door opens itself to me. I notice a figure that has the ability to take my breath away.

Ellie exhales sharply and rubs her thighs as she remains seated on my porch steps. Her gray Nirvana T-shirt matches the paint on the house, and her nude lipstick and curled hair drag a green goblin out of me. Ellie gets to be pretty and go out for more than just court dates. Ellie has people who still want to be seen with her in public. Ellie doesn't have to hide. But Ellie takes the time out of her day to see Hope and me. "Hey."

I take a seat next to her, and then it dawns on me—where is Hope? "Hey. Did you—"

"Yeah. I heard, so I skipped my glamorous night out and stayed with her."

My head tilts to the side. "How? I mean, how'd you hear?"

"Amy's magic eraser won't stop me from realizing that my best friend might need a bit of help." Her voice softens. "So I'm here to help. I brought pizza and lava cakes to soothe the blues whenever you're up for eating."

"Hope?"

"Fed. And asleep. Now talk to me."

"I don't even know where to start."

"Court? We can start there. TMZ caught you storming out, and your face—you looked like you had seen a ghost or something."

A scratchiness in my throat appears as I try to focus on the shrubs that were planted by someone who wasn't me. There were blooming petals there once. I guess they died off after I moved here. "Evelyn—" Ellie's initial reaction screams *I told you so*, but instead she says nothing. "I knew it wouldn't be easy. I just don't understand why we're going this far."

"What do you mean?" Ellie questioned.

"This whole fucking court case! I'm sure recordings are all over the internet like it's some sick joke by now. But I'm fucking terrified, El! Because it's not a joke. It's not a meme. It's not a stupid fucking video to just throw on Twitter and laugh at. It's my life. And right now I really wish I was anyone but myself. I wish I was anywhere else but here."

"I know that I'm the new friend that came with this new world and that what I say doesn't matter all that much."

I exhale as my body tenses in preparation for the lecture. There are times where I don't need her to tell me how to fix my problems but instead just listen. Aly was always a great listener.

"But I want you to know that whatever has been going on in that head of yours, I'm willing to listen to. You didn't ask for this bullshit, and if I would have met you before you got tied in with Xavier fucking Amari, I would have dragged you so far away from it."

I bite the inside of my lip. "I know. And I want to tell you so much, but I just . . . Things are so different now. And I don't really know if I've even grasped it all. It—it feels like I'm not all the way here . . . most times."

"You're a mother now, and the father of your child isn't here anymore. I don't expect the world from you. I just want to help."

I consciously blink for the first time in days. With my eyes closed, I notice a road that leads to the hill. I'm almost at one hundred miles per hour, and I'm going so fast that it feels like flying. "I can see it now." I slowly open my eyes.

"Huh?"

I cast a tight smile in Ellie's direction. "Nothing. What were you saying?"

"I was on Instagram, and one of those blogs said that the car had no license plate and that the owner was an unidentified male." She exaggerates the word *male* while looking straight at me. "Going sixty miles an hour and missed the cliff by like three inches. Ran right into a tree. How much of that is true?"

"Oh." I purse my lips in an attempt to get back on the same page with her. "All of it except . . . I was going a hundred miles an hour."

Ellie pulls a piece of hair behind her ear before laughing ironically. "I'm sorry. No. You were not." The laughter continues and only makes me want to crawl into a hole and die. "I'm sorry! But look, you would be dead. Flung through your windshield and dead, Arlissa. Do you hear me?"

"No. No." I shake my head enough times to trigger a minor headache. The pulsing intensifies, and everything about my friend begins to blur. "The numbers . . . The numbers right in front of me said I was going up to a hundred."

I can feel her hand finding its way onto my back and moving up and down with caution. "No, Arlissa. You weren't. There's just no way you were even going past the speed limit. The highway up to that hill is a damn speed trap. Cops are always patrolling. You would have been pulled over."

"Oh."

What is my truth then? There are three sides to every story: hers, mine, and what really happened. When did my truth stop aligning with reality? How do I make my own voice credible again?

You cry.

My body jolts. God, I wish he'd announce himself.

Stop being the victim, and make other people be your victim. Honestly, it shouldn't have even taken you this long to figure that much out.

The tears begin to stream down my face like I had prepared for this my entire life.

Be clear who the leaders are and who the followers are. May you live as long as you want and never want as long as you live.

"I don't think I'm going to make it through this."

She squeezes my shoulder.

Oop! You got her.

"Sometimes we have to do things we don't want to, to survive."

"Like surviving?"

"Exactly like surviving. The only way out is through."

"Well, fuck that. It feels like I'm walking through fire."

"Then put on a fireproof suit, and you walk, okay? Because I won't let you lose yourself. You'll walk out of this a hero." She smirks, pulling at my sweatshirt. "Hopefully, a way better dressed hero."

Maybe Ellie is onto something. Maybe Xavier is too. I can be everything that I'm scared of. "You think so?"

"I know so. This doesn't have to haunt you forever, Lissa. And they will see that it was a suicide. You are someone worth admiring. Not someone to be outcast like their bad decisions define them. What was the worst thing you did to him? Love the bastard? Stand there while he got so high he'd punch you for just asking him how his dad was? You birthed his child, and you are the strongest woman on earth for that one, babe."

I nod. Because she's one hundred percent correct. I meet these people, and they watch me take in all of their trauma and flaws until I'm an oversoaked sponge that can no longer be used. They allow me to soak it all in and then toss me to the side while I collect dust and grow mold because I've become a walking reminder of them. I will no longer be that. I will no longer think three times about when it's appropriate to open up my eyes. I tried a million times, but there is no way to go quietly. What do you do when you say "I love you" and no one hears you? What do you do when other people convince themselves that you're the problem? You stand up, and you wipe the expression of shock off of their sorry faces when you get what you're owed.

Hope's restlessness isn't the main factor that keeps me up tonight. Instead, it's closing my eyes and only seeing the images of people who have made me feel small. It begins with Xavier and ends with a reflection of myself.

My left hand crosses over my torso as I peel the sheets off of my small frame. I can't wake her. I turn my head to the occupied bassinet near the wall. The room is pitch black, but when I tiptoe over to her, even in the darkest of nights her sunshine illuminates around her. Her arms aloft as if she's dreaming of breakfast and my ten thousand kisses on her cheeks before noon.

I caress her cheek with the back of my hand, and with every knuckle that touches her skin that's as soft as rose petals, I promise my heart to only her. *Outside.* Globs of spit fall to the back of my throat with every step I take out of the bedroom. I quickly grab a bottle of wine off of the bar we created by just placing bottles in the corner of the kitchen counter. My shorts and T-shirt will have to do. I stare at my phone plugged in on the kitchen table and head over to it. I press the power button in order to check the time: 5:45. The phone can stay where it is. I won't need it where I'm going. One foot goes into the rubber sandals and then the other. Before throwing myself out of the door, I find a pair of sunglasses just in case.

The walk is quick, but not quick enough. I feel the concrete sidewalk of my neighborhood for the first time in a year. I watch the houses as the moon tries its best to show them to me. The perfectly cut lawns, the silent streets, and not a single person knows I'm out here. I even take a moment to listen for the squirrels. Not a single rustle of the leaves. Eager fingers wrestle the foil top off of the glass bottle, and I tilt my head back in preparation to chug. Ellie and I lose the corks to our tequila more often than I'm willing to admit. I crumple the thin metal and let it hit the ground. Fuck the earth if it's trying to put me in prison for falling in love with a psycho.

The grass fields become visible to me at the same time that the sun does. As the grass gets taller, I walk straight through it. I let the itchiness of the earth irritate my skin from my toes to my knees and just keep chugging. The alcohol punches its way down my throat and lights a fire in my belly. It rumbles and it roars, and the smoke it creates doesn't escape out of my mouth or nose. No. It goes straight to my brain and causes my steps to go from steady to unbalanced. This tequila is the amber that lights up my soul.

I gulp, looking down at the now empty bottle. "I know I was going up to a hundred." The words fall out of my lips before I can catch them. Frustration builds as the lingering burning sensation of the liquid lingers. Why is everyone trying to make me feel crazy? My right hand squeezes the bottle harder than I thought I was capable of. The sky begins to dance with splashes of orange and purple. The moon takes the backseat, and all it does is hurt. I've got every right to hurt inside. I know I do. But that doesn't mean I have to be a victim. "I know you cheated."

Tears fall organically this time, and I hate every moment of it. Without warning, a loud shriek forces itself out of my mouth at the same time that the bottle goes from in my hand to shattered somewhere in the field. I keep screaming, my body folding into itself as it releases every deep-seated emotion that's been there for one month too long. I'm angry at what I did. I'm angry that I'm terrified of facing it. I'm angry that I'm a mother to a child who will never know her father no matter how twisted he was. I'm angry that I lost my best friend over a man that I never actually wanted.

"Do you see me now, asshole?" I shout into the sky. The birds fly over my head as the sun continues to push itself into its highest position in the sky. A rustle in the grass causes my body to fall to the ground while I frantically search around for the source of it.

"I hear you." He speaks, crouching down to a level that my drunken eyes can process. He's dressed differently again. This time in his normal T-shirt and Nike shorts like he's about to go for a run. His tan skin is a complete one-eighty to the pale state that I've been forced to remember him as.

"Well, good! 'Cause I've got a lot to say to you."

He reaches his hand out in order to help me get back on two feet. The alcohol is starting to lead me down a dangerous road of inebriation.

He crosses his arms like he always did when he waited for me to say something ridiculous. At least this time he's not squeezing my hand. "Go ahead, tell me."

"What? No. It's never been that easy for you. It can't be now. Are you fucking kidding me?"

Xavier chuckles before shaking his head. "Okay, sorry. You want me to put up a fight? We can fight! But we all know how badly that ended last time. Or do you?" He paces back and forth, the grass bending to his every whim.

I suck my teeth. "What are you going to do? Tell me some stupid story about how I can't trust my own brain?"

"No. Because you already know that. You know that I'm not really standing here, but you also know that you want bodies to stop dropping every decade and a half around you, and you don't know where to start."

"Start with what?" It becomes harder to focus. I pinch myself to make sure I'm awake. I just need to feel something. Ouch. Okay.

"Figure out how you started talking to ghosts. Oh, we can try figuring out how my mom is playing you."

"So since you know everything . . . where do I start?"

"The beginning."

Chapter

ELEVEN

*M*y mother was never the nurturing type. If you asked a question, you should have known the answer, regardless if no one taught you. In her mind, your school system and her school system from fifty-something years ago are exactly the same. She learned to cook at fifteen, so why weren't you born with the skill even though you've never cooked a day in your life? Why are you burning the chicken even though you watched her make it that one time on Thanksgiving? You should have known. Oh, and it has to be exactly how she likes it, or it doesn't make sense. Google it, ask someone else, risk it; but don't ever let her see you try. Only let her see you ace it, because if not you're a dumbass who should have known from birth. Her brain works differently than everyone else's; at least that's how my dad would describe it. She was *(and* *still is)* mentally sharp. But the disconnect comes from her assuming everyone else thinks the same way she does.

"Where'd you go last night?" Ellie reeks of disappointment while standing in the doorway. The last thing I remember? Passing out in the grass and waking up to an ant crawling on my arm. Didn't she leave? I don't remember her leaving. Has she been here the entire time?

There's this saying my mom used to talk about—smoke and mirrors. It doesn't matter what is. It only matters what people think.

I scratch my head and go straight for the coffeepot. "Where's Hope?" I question, pouring the liquid into the cup that I'll probably just stir with a spoon until it's cold.

I can't remember how Mrs. Kenya Benson acted prior to Samantha dying. But I know once she did, there was no reasoning with her. I learned to experience life alone and depend on the kindness of strangers. I stopped asking questions and started taking risks. I only told her when I was absolutely proud of myself and never told her when I was unsure. I envied the girls on teen drama TV who would tell their mothers they were pregnant, and they'd hug them and say that they were there for them. Clearly disappointed, but they would work through that together. My mother would never react that way.

In fact, there was a time where I was failing a class, and the school called her. Failing wasn't like me, so they just wanted to check in, see what was going on. She slapped me so hard my earrings fell out. They were hoops with rose quartz in the middle. I had bought them when going to see some national monument that I can't remember the name of for a school trip. I watched a stone that I thought was supposed to bring love into my life fall onto the ground. I don't know who picked it up, but it wasn't me. For years after, I wondered how she did that and not a single soul heard or saw. Or if they did, not said anything.

I blamed my mother's behavior on grief. Plus, when we were good, we were super good! She was my best friend, and I guess that's where the lines got tangled, because now we don't speak. But I don't like to dwell on that. When you can pay your own bills, there's really nothing that ties you to your parents. You can go off the grid and ghost them like anyone else in this world.

"We need to talk." She takes a few steps toward me.

"I don't think we do. I just need to know where she is so I can get her bottle ready and have one calm day."

My mother taught me two things within the last few years without saying a word. One, I wouldn't be a good parent because I've never experienced one. Two, Xavier and I were super-duper similar. Amy never laid a finger on him, I don't think. But she didn't mind when his dad did since they wanted the same things in the end. Is that what makes a marriage or a parent? Having an end goal for another human being and that end goal being them benefiting your own personal legacy? I should have asked him more about it. I never did, though.

"Arlissa, where were you?" Ellie snaps and crosses her arms over her chest.

"I went on a walk!"

"For four hours? I woke up, and you were gone!" Hope must be awake, because Ellie is content with showcasing her disappointment by raising her voice.

"Yes, El," I say crossly. "Sometimes, when in mourning or, I don't know . . . Caring for a newborn in the midst of the biggest murder trial in the fucking United States can get a little stressful. So yes. I took a walk."

"I-I—" She stammers a bit before getting it together. "I'm sorry. I know it's been hard—"

"No, no. It's fine. I'll just deal with it all some other way. Oh, I know! I'll take up golf." I roll my eyes and grab a bottle out of the fridge. I grab it with both hands and put it in front of my crotch. With one fair swing, I aim my imaginary golf club at her face. "Oh! Hole in one."

"Wait." There's a pleading glimmer in Ellie's eyes, one I only see when she's sober. It shows in the way she subtly leans forward or the way she squints only enough to get a peak behind the windows of my soul.

Ellie always had a perfect family. Not sure how, but they supported her. It's what I envy most about her, actually. She's never carried the same kind of traumas and memories that we do. She chose to dye her hair different colors, while the rest of her family went to church and wore pencil skirts and slacks. She made the decision to cling onto cocaine and heroin for reasons I don't fucking know. She has the perfect life, the perfect boyfriend, and for some reason she's hell-bent on killing herself.

Unlike Aly, Xavier, and me, Ellie's momma loves her. I mean, I know ours did (or do) too in their own odd way. But her mom treats her with respect and puts her on every pedestal possible. Her dad too. Ellie is the queen of her family, a golden retriever in a room of mutts, if you will. They support her music career, and daddy's money makes it possible for her to own multiple properties like this one. But you see, the thing with Ellie is she's a hero. Always has been.

"What?"

"Before you go in there, I need to tell you something." Her low tone exaggerates the word *need* and causes me to raise a brow.

When I found out I was pregnant, I called her. Well, and also Christian. And then I tried to call Bailey, but she must have changed her phone number. See, I can't say exactly why I chose to do that. But Ellie came because one heroic flaw is that they are compelled by this need to be there for anyone and everyone. Especially in Ellie's case, because she won't even question it if she loves you.

Christian wanted to come and convince me that we could do this together and maybe the baby was his. Somehow. Some way. I think he's just as delusional as I am.

I push past the woman and blatantly ignore the warning signs in her stance, glare, and clenched jaw. The hall feels unfamiliar, and a draft coming from the vent above me is more distinguishable than before. The halls are blank. A single stock photo of a flower is framed by the bedroom door, but it ends there. Taking family photos always felt weird. Ellie mentioned it once, but it only made me cry. I think she knows she's always going to be the hero she wanted to be to me. But that's the problem with being a hero, you are always just that. A person who gets someone out of a terrible situation, but you can't give them back what they lost. She makes it easier to put a smile where a less honest frown belongs. But she's not even half of who Aly is. And now I have to watch her play godmother to Savannah's son instead.

I turn the corner, registering Ellie's light footsteps catching up behind me before I can fully understand what my eyes are seeing. Her usual curled blond tresses are bone straight. Piercing blue eyes dressed with crow's feet catch my youthful brown ones, and all I can do is stare. Bloodless and wrinkled pale hands grip onto Hope's powder-blue blanket, yet it feels like what she's gripping onto are my lungs.

I need someone to tell me how to feel, because my brain is scattering a mile a minute, and it's holding hands with my quickening breath. My heart is thumping out of my chest as if a bomb is about to go off, and I'm sure it's written on my face. Of course it is, because she's smiling.

"Good morning, Arlissa."

"Put her down," I push out.

She stands and keeps Hope close to her chest, who is currently lying in the older woman's arms with no intention of reacting to the situation. How could she? She's only been on this earth a few months.

"Well, that's a rude way to say good morning."

"Put her down."

"Arlissa . . ." Ellie interrupts from behind me, but I can't muster up enough confidence in Amy to take my eyes off of her.

"Shut up," I command and raise my hand up so that she fully gets the picture.

This is her fault, you know.

Amy chuckles and gently bounces Hope. "Oh, bless your heart." The passive-aggressive tone comes out like hot lava—burning to the touch.

"How—"

"No." Her cocky smirk falls instantly as she turns to place Hope gently on the bed.

I want to run and grab her, but my feet feel nailed to

the wood floors. Instead, I just stand there helplessly and focus on gulping down the immense amount of spit that's puddling in my mouth.

"You see, you don't get to command things or ask the questions anymore. In fact, you don't get to do anything." Amy folds her trench-coat-covered arms over her chest and takes a single step toward me. "Did you really think you could keep my grandchild from me?"

"She—"

"Aht! Sh . . ." She brings her pointer finger up to her lips. I focus on how the red on her mouth matches with the red on her nails. "You took all that time insinuating that I, me, am the worst mother on earth. Yet somehow you fell in what you'd like to call love with a product of my parenting. Which obviously means it wasn't that horrible, right? He gave you luxury, comfort beyond your wildest dreams, and against my wishes he went for you anyway."

"Your wishes?"

Go back to the beginning. Make her.

"What?"

"Oh, darling. You were never made for any of this. Well, I assumed so. Now, with how conniving you've been, I'd like to think I've underestimated you. My son had a sickness inside of him, and it had nothing to do with pressure or pain or how he was raised. No, he was born with this sickness, and it was called passion, falling, if you will." She sits herself on the bed, crossing her right leg over her left and flashing the red bottoms of her boots. The boots I know she paid for with Xavier's blood. "When he was a child, he had this habit of striking up these conversations with our waitresses. If he found one to be pretty, he'd stare at her until she offered him more crayons or another apple juice. But no. My Xavier wanted a conversation. He wanted to know her. And if they pulled up a chair and talked to him—which they always would, might I add—he'd draw them. Did you know he could draw?"

"No."

"Of course not. Well, he used to all the time before he found a new love—boxing."

"You mean before he was beaten into loving it?"

A roar of laughter so loud she has to cover her own mouth comes from Amy. "Oh, I hope you didn't plan on raising a child with a brain like that!"

I raise a brow and ignore the sweat beads developing on my forehead.

"Xavier was never forced to box. He simply chose to. His father told him how he'd train him. He told him that it was either this or becoming a less than favorable artist. A painter who can't face his own work, even. He was not abused. In fact, he was rather spoiled if you ask me."

"He was beaten until he fought back."

She shrugs. "My boy was a natural-born pacifist. Anyway, I told you to stop talking. Now where was I? Oh, right. You weren't the only woman he brought to my doorstep begging for me to take in. Savannah was the first, but in his defense, she was the best choice after all. She never got too loud or embarrassed us. She sure as hell didn't cause this much of a stir. And when she decided that he was as stupid a boy as any, she made her quiet escape. Now she's someone else's daughter-in-law. He kept seeing her, you know. When you two started and finished and started and finished . . ." She rolls her eyes. "She'd always pop up at one point. Do you know why, Arlissa? Because it's never been you."

The words sting more than anything else she could have said. The idea of Savannah being anything close to what Xavier needed makes my skin crawl. I know Xavier saw me as a frantic woman—a girl even. A child who was terrified of short conversations and crowded places. But he took a chance on me. He would always look me in the eyes and make me feel like mine were a brightly burning hazel too. He told me that he'd take me home. He told me that he would teach me. He looked at me and knew that I only wanted to hold him. I thought he wanted to only hold me too.

Whenever he wasn't boxing for a long period of time, I got to see him in a different light. Those were the times where I wanted to share spaces with him, where I wasn't hindered by performance anxiety. We'd lie on the floor and daydream about what a future looked like, but most importantly, felt like. Even when he messed with my head, even when he looked me in the eye and said he didn't want to see me anymore, those were the only times I felt like I made a mistake.

"You were nothing to him. You gave him nothing, you couldn't even make him smile. Don't you get that?"

"Amy . . ." Ellie steps up.

"Remember what I told you, girl." She snaps before her attention comes back to me.

Xavier introduced me to the crazy idea of facing your fears by pushing me off of cliffs that looked too dangerous from afar. And at the end of every hasty decision, he'd turn to me and tell me: "See? You didn't die." And he wasn't wrong. But Amy is.

"You were a charity case, my dear. One I wish I could

prevent from happening, but we can't go back in time, now can we?"

With every word, she attempts to break my spirit, but instead I bask in the warm light of the memories she can't touch. I go into the deepest part of my mind that fills me with a euphoric warmth that drugs never measured up to. I couldn't ask for more from a lover. He gave me diamonds and a movie-screen love. He gave me bruises that left me crying on the bathroom floor. In exchange for his life, he gave me my lust for life back. I won't be broken down, because Amy can't put my fire out. There's one thing she's missing, and that's the person that Xavier built. When I'm hurt, I only get stronger.

"So, you are going to have some quiet time in this little safehouse you've conquered for yourself. And don't bother wondering how I found you; that'd be useless. Just focus on what matters." Amy stands and grabs Hope, who I'm just now realizing is fully dressed. She bends down and picks up her baby bag and hikes it over her shoulder.

"What are you doing?"

"Oh? Did you think I was going to leave this baby with you? No, no. My grandchild deserves better than that." All of my fears begin rushing up to the surface. "It seems you've lost your vision. I am the one who is keeping that behind of yours out of prison. I hired your darling lawyer, and just as fast as I gave her to you, I can snatch her back." The woman steps into my space, and the fear of crowded rooms crumbles me as if there's nowhere else to go. "What did I tell you about secrets, Arlissa? I told you I don't like them. Almost as much as I don't like that you killed my son."

I'm frozen. She's walking toward the door, and I can't even chase her. I watch as she takes my angel further and further away from me. Yet it's when she reaches for the doorknob that the spell she had on me wears off.

"Stop!" I shout, tears filling in my ducts. "Please. Bring her back."

Amy doesn't even stop. Instead she swings the door open to reveal a black car parked outside. Was that always there? Why didn't I notice?

"Bring her back!" I fling my body forward, but I'm immediately caught by Ellie's weak embrace. But somehow it's enough to slow me down.

"I'm sorry," she mumbles while I kick and scream as hard as I can. Amy steps outside, not even looking behind her. Hope doesn't even open her eyes to look over Amy's shoulder. I wish she was old enough to fight. I wish she was old enough to reach out for me.

"Hope!" I scream, focusing on trying to wiggle out of Ellie's grip. My kicks do nothing. She doesn't even flinch. Why isn't she moving? She's not that big. "Get off of me!" Fire-hot tears fall down my cheeks while I'm tortured with the sight of watching Amy nonchalantly buckle my daughter into a car seat. My daughter. "I'm going to kill you, you fucking bitch! I swear to God, I'm going to kill you like I killed your fucking son!"

I can see a smirk appear on her features, and it isn't until she's safe in the passenger seat of the vehicle that Ellie lets go of me.

I sprint out of the house immediately. "I promise!" I shout, my legs weakening, and my body gets covered by the smoke of the engine while the car pulls off.

You can't chase her down, not now.

A desperate shriek starts at my belly and rushes out of my mouth.

"I promise . . ." I whisper in between breaths while my knees hit the concrete in the street.

Chapter
TWELVE

When Samantha died, I used to over-play the pain. I told people I would have shot back if I was given a gun. Or that I personally knew Ebony Gilinsky, who bailed last minute and missed out on the grand massacre at the Marvelous Quincy Movie Theater. I ran into her once at a Berlin Film Festival that Ellie had dragged me to as her plus-one. I didn't have Xavier there to kick me in the ass and tell me to get it together. She told me she had a copy of my Cosmo shoot on her coffee table. I froze.

But no matter how far I travel through the filing cabinet of my memories, I can't find a time I was strong enough to handle this. Losing Samantha was a tragedy that friends and family had to see me go through. Losing Xavier was a devastating event that strangers watched me go through. Yet I've lost Hope in private. So how am I engulfed in embarrassment?

I am the worst version of myself.

My eyes scan the bedroom, looking for an escape, a way out. It's emptier now that Ellie has left. I don't know where she is. I don't care.

I take quiet steps over to the bathroom, keeping my arms wrapped as tightly around myself as possible. I grasp onto my own body in a desperate attempt to replicate the chemicals that release when you hug someone you love. Except I'm not hugging a person I love. With every step, I feel Xavier taking my hand, guiding me to turn on the light, the water next. My nostrils fill with his expensive shampoo that smells of sweet grass. I watch as the bathtub fills, feeling smaller than every molecule that makes up the water. The wings he provided me are gone, burned off with every bad decision that was made, but without them I have nothing. Without them, I'm no taller than the secrets I choose not to acknowledge.

It's easier with someone or something to throw the blame on. Yet in this bathroom with a six-foot mirror, there's only me. If I point a finger, it goes back to me.

Once the water reaches its peak, I shut it off. He's here once again. I close my eyes to get the full picture. He's smiling, guiding me into the tub and telling me that I don't have to take anything off. I'm okay as I am. I follow his guidance, hoping that he'll take me wherever he goes. I remember the first time he took my hand, and I followed him no matter what. I knew from that day that I'd follow him six feet under if I had to. I envisioned his palm meeting mine when I pushed Hope out in that bathtub—I think.

I remember when every word that fell off of his lips were bible to me, like when he said forever. If someone would have told me that he was lying then, I'd tell them they were insane. If someone would have told me that I'd be lying in bed alone again, I'd call them crazy. And they'd all be calling me right now to say I told you so.

Alejandra loved saying she told me so. I wonder if she has to correct Savannah's behavior as much as she corrected mine. It hurts to admit, but they make a good pair. I'll sneak on social media sometimes and see they did a high-quality photoshoot in Vegas. Just two besties with matching pumps and the same Birkins in different colors. Do they talk about me?

My socks get soaked first, then my jeans, and my sweater. I can feel the heavy fabric gripping my chest, weighing me down with every drop of water it soaks up. I sit there, hoping for it to get heavier and heavier in order to mimic the touch that I crave more than air itself. If I try hard enough, if I shut off every practical sense, I can mimic Hope and Xavier lying on my chest. From the neck down, I'm submerged in the warmth of the steady water that's waiting for me to make a move before it does. I keep my eyes closed, visualizing that it's his arms instead of the empty liquid I'm currently engulfed in. To touch him right now, I'd give the air in my lungs. To love him right now, I'd give my sight away. To have the family I deserve, I'd bleed out eternally.

No one asks how I'm feeling. Instead, they jump the gun and tell me to go screw myself because I'm a murderous bitch, and when I close my eyes, I see myself in an insane asylum. I'm being pumped with drugs and told to wake up, but I don't want to wake up.

Sometimes problems happen and I can't do anything to stop it. I deal with things accordingly. I always have. Why does the public care? I'm the only one who deals with it in the end, anyway. If everyone would understand that and do me a fucking solid and stop commenting their think-pieces in blog comments and social media captions—that'd be nice.

They're right, though. Okay, that's true. But if everything has been taken from me, can I at least have my problems to myself? Does everyone else want a piece of that too?

I remember when we'd dance to no music playing, even when we hung out with his friends. They'd laugh and tell us to get a room, but they just didn't understand. I miss that. I miss calling his name and listening to it echo down the halls—and even better, his replies. I want it all back. I'd give anything to have it back. God, take everything. Please.

I made a mistake. There, I said it. But it wasn't my fault . . . I swear it! I'm sorry, I know I sound angry. I'm not. I promise.

"I need you," I whisper, a hot tear escaping from my eye and mixing with the water. I make believe that he's hovering over me, running his fingers through my curls like he used to. Calmer than usual. Sweeter than usual. I want to reach out, but my hands know better than that. I don't feel haunted, I feel blessed. But as he sits there, I want to beg for forgiveness. As his sweet features look down at me and his breath lingers over my forehead, I pray he forgives me. Maybe if I join him, he will.

"I'm sorry," I finally say, but I know in my heart there won't be any forgiveness until I come to terms with the truth. What kind of mother am I if I don't own up to the things that ripped her from my arms in the first place? Am I a mother at all? If I'm a mother with no child, does that only make me an empty woman?

Admit it.

I slide deeper into the warmth, hoping to drown him out. The strands that once held weight on top of my head begin to lose any amount of mass. They turn weightless, as do I. I don't focus on holding my breath. It's easier to stop breathing that way. Just let it go.

We had just gotten back together. You've got to understand, emotions have never been easy for me. I know, I've only tried a handful of times to detach from the tortures that sprout from my brain. It's never worked! People still look at me like I'm fucking crazy. Maybe . . . Maybe I never really tried.

You got upset . . . We had just tried for Hope, and you freaked! I just wanted you to shut up. I wanted you to stop screaming, stop calling me fucking stupid. I wanted it to end, but only for a moment. I didn't want you to not wake up. You told me you'd kill me when you did because you were so upset. I was scared!

Before sleeping, I turned into someone unrecognizable. I crushed the sleeping pills I knew were too strong. I told you we could have a drink and go to bed. It was a long night. I didn't remember it fully until months later. I kept my hands to myself the first hour. Then you fell asleep. You fell asleep, and you were sleeptalking. You said you hated me. You said that in your sleep. I was going to let that go!

I looked through your phone.

I shouldn't have looked through your phone.

Savannah. Vanessa.

I don't remember grabbing the knife.

I don't remember forgetting how much I love you.

I love you.

I love you.

I swear.

It's a spiritual euphoria when I think of you.

I was scared. I didn't want to get left behind.

Forgive me.

If I stay down here, it can all go away. We'll be able to meet again, and the fresh memories I have of you will remain just that—fresh. The last kiss, it sits on my lips as I use the water to replicate the feeling. The memories aren't good enough. It still causes a sharp pain to my chest. It'll all be over, and there will be nothing to be forgiven for. Hope will go to a private school, and she's a girl; she won't have to box. Maybe she'll sing and be bigger than Aly. All the bad will fade away, and I'll have real wings. I'll be with the only person who knows me, and I won't have to worry about something so sweet becoming a haunting figure in my nightmares.

I have a secret greater than the one that played out that night. It's that I know I'll never get over you. It's no longer clear who's haunting who.

In my mind, I'm standing on a cliff. He's supposed to be here, I'm listening for a footstep, for a sign. I turn around and he's there. The chill of the wind quickly pauses at the sight of him. He's just as tall, just as electrifying. I'm with him again. I allow my fingers to trace every ink-drawn line on his arms. He takes my hand, leading my weightless body to the edge of the cliff. He's trying to take me somewhere new. Somewhere only he's seen, like every other time before.

Jump.

I could have this forever if I really wanted. Amy can be a better mother than I ever would have dreamed of.

What if I jump and I hug you for the first time in

forever, but it still doesn't release that chemical? What if admitting that was all for nothing? What if our love was never as sacred as I dreamed it to be, but instead the holy ground I craved came from a child who has done nothing less than give me strength? It's not you, Xavier.

It's her.

My reflexes kick in and push me out of the hold the water has on me. I take a huge gasp of air, lifting my hands up to wipe the water out of my face. They're shaking, and for the first time in months, I'm looking at them and not envisioning bloodstains. Being broken inside is always described as an internal feeling, but I promise it seems like every bone in my body is crushed. I'm losing my fucking mind.

Lately, I've hated myself. I'm done pointing fingers at anyone but me.

My eyes peer open to a tiny spider hanging in front of me. It doesn't freak out. It becomes invisible. The spider doesn't initiate contact with me; it's still as I am still. If I try to kill it, it'll try to run. It must be planning an escape— just in case. Like I should be doing. It doesn't make the first move—it only reacts.

Chapter
THIRTEEN

She types frantically in her office while I make my way through the law firm. Cyrus Law. Easy to remember and straight to the point. Of course she owns her own firm, but if she's that good, why is she throwing my case? I pass massive potted plants placed in random corners and a receptionist's desk that I happily disregard. I'm sure the woman assigned to that dreadful job is wondering why I didn't stop—I don't care.

I tried a thousand times to excuse the obvious bullshit circling me this entire time. I'm done, I'm tired. I'm going to be the passive-aggressive one for a change.

I push open the massive glass door and take in every surprised and disapproving look her eyes shoot in my direction. Her office is huge, practically the size of the place I'm living in now. I remember when rooms this big were my norm. If things were different, would I have had my own agency with an office this large? Her midnight-black desk reflects the sunlight coming from the window behind her. Underneath my brown pumps is a gray rug that's probably worth more than I've spent all year.

Evelyn slowly shuts her laptop and leans back in what has to be a very comfortable office chair. I take a seat as well and place my purse on her desk.

"Did the paparazzi see you? I thought we discussed minimizing public appearances, especially after that show you put on in front of the courthouse."

"We did."

"So?"

I shrug. "I don't know," I say in between small giggles. "I didn't listen."

"And why not?"

"Because it's bullshit. What is being quiet getting me? Seriously. What?"

Evelyn clears her throat and glances at her phone, but she doesn't touch it. "What can I do for you today, Arlissa?"

"Who is testifying next?"

"We have an entire preparation for that scheduled tomorrow, but if you must know now, it's Savannah Middleton."

Irritation is written all over my features. Why not anyone else? "What the hell does she have to say?"

"She's an eyewitness to both yours and Xavier's character. The prosecution thinks she'll be a good witness for them."

My shoulders tense, and I sit up in the chair in pure disbelief. "And what about our witnesses?"

Evelyn's eyes dart around the room for a moment, as if she's trying to think of some con to feed me next. "We don't have much to work with. No offense, but there isn't a single person you know who can speak in favor of you. I've called around. I've tried. But no one wants to speak in your favor."

"That's bullshit."

She leans back in her seat. "Why are we even speaking about this now? You could have called."

I roll my eyes. "If you would have answered the phone when I did call, I wouldn't have had to make this trip. I have to get back to Hope." I force a smile and try to cover the shivers down my spine as the lies pour out of my mouth.

Evelyn's bushy brows briefly knit together, but she corrects it just as fast. "I've been busy."

What is she hiding?

"With what? I'm your only fucking client."

"I own an entire firm, Arlissa, and unfortunately you're not the only criminal in town," she snaps.

I exhale and rest my hand under my bed of curls as I try my best not to slap her right then and there. She's bullshitting me. I know she is. But about what? "Fine, I'll make this quick. Change your approach. I said no fucking insanity plea, and what do you do? You start painting this picture that I'm nuts. Do you think I'm stupid?"

"Listen, you watch your mouth." Evelyn rises from her seat and grips her hands onto the edge of the desk.

"No. You watch your mouth. Because Madison has been working overtime to change this narrative you aided in putting into the world. I'm not crazy! And I'm not going to let whoever gets up on that stand next tell me I am. He killed himself." I scoff. "You're the crazy one if you think I'm gonna let you wreck this train. I am not going to jail.

And if you're going to try and put me on a grippy sock trip, you've got no idea who you're talking to. Fix it. Or I will."

"I am doing the best I can for an impossible case. You would know if you cared to pay attention to any of our prep meetings."

Impossible. No, it's not. "Whatever. I'll see you first thing tomorrow." I sharply inhale and force a smile on my features, hoping she thinks she won.

I don't give her an option to challenge any of my claims. Or give her time to formulate a ridiculous reason for why I'm wrong and she's right. Instead, I reposition my bag on my shoulders and head straight for the door that's too heavy to pull open in a fit of rage. "Nice rug," I mutter in between using all my strength to get the door wide enough to squeeze through.

Something is off. I can't trust her, no way. I quickly head to the elevator and press the down button more times than necessary. The machine dings, and the metal doors slide open to reveal an empty box. A sigh of relief leaves my matte nude lips while I step in. Once they close, I unlock my phone and head straight to the recently dialed.

Are you sure?

I roll my eyes at his tone. He doesn't trust me. I don't blame him, though. My one blue nail taps on the number, and the call starts. It rings a few times, four, now five.

"This is the California office for *The City Talks*. How can I help you?"

"Hello. This is Arlissa Benson. Do you have a journalist available for a meeting?"

Chapter
FOURTEEN

No one wants to speak in your favor. The words bounced around my brain all night. It has to be a lie. There has to be someone on this earth who can speak in my favor. I'm not a bad person. I'm not crazy.

I'm not crazy.

I'm not crazy.

I'm not— "All rise!"

I wish I still did drugs. Coke. Any drug, really. I'd be in better spirits than I am right now. I can't take the lows, though. They consist of nightmares, and the voices aren't maintainable. There was a time when I never heard them, I think. Those days are getting further and further away, but the memories still exist. Time is funny like that, glorification of the past while somehow looking forward to the future. Things changed when Samantha spoke to me for the first time. I thought I was slowly dying while simultaneously trying to live—kind of like she did in her last moments.

Savannah's not on the stand yet. I watch my surroundings like a hawk as if she's going to magically appear. I wonder, is stealing Alejandra my karma for taking Xavier from her? It'd make sense if it is. I don't blame her.

She has a son now. She doesn't care to worry about you, Xavier chimes in. I search the room discreetly for his presence, but there's nothing, only the echoes in my head.

I'm not crazy.

I grip tightly onto this uncomfortable chair. Reporters are here; I can't look so on edge. God, why did I say I didn't know who she was? And now she's at my trial. Of course I know who she is. I'm an idiot. They can use it against me. Evelyn was right. I should have listened. I mean, hell. Maybe I am losing it.

No. Don't give up, baby sis. You can't give up. You need to get your daughter back.

Oh, come on. You know my mother wouldn't hurt her grandchild. Give it up. You take the plea, you're out in a few years, and if you're lucky you'll make it to her first day of school.

Lissa, if you're going to go away regardless, why don't you go down fighting? You made a mistake.

The mistake being killing me, but yeah! Let's yell and shout and make a big fucking scene!

Make them see you, Lissa. Like they did when I was taken from you.

I throw my head into my hands in a desperate attempt to make them stop. If I scream, they're locking me away and throwing out the key. Haven't I gone through enough?

The courtroom feels different today. More reporters than usual, sure. But somehow it feels emptier. Like everyone here is waiting for something to happen that doesn't revolve around me. I used to catch a juror or two staring at me periodically, but now it's like they couldn't care less. The guy who sits near the front with his notepad is usually fixated on my facial expressions—fixated on me. But no one is anymore. They're all staring at the stand.

"Are you ready to call your first witness for the day, Ms. Baker?"

The prosecutor commands the attention of everyone in the room by standing. "Our only witness for the day, Judge. Dr. Leghal could not make it to court today."

"Well, get him to court, because that's another day added."

"Yes, Judge. Today I will be calling Savannah Middleton to the stand."

My stomach ties itself in knots as fear washes over me. My lungs collapse as if the wind has been knocked out of them while large hands squeeze my throat until my pulse gives out. They squeeze and then allow me a half second of release. They squeeze and only release when I'm about to pass out. God, I can't fucking breathe.

The wooden doors are being pulled open by the guards, I'm sure. I can't see. I refuse to look behind me. I hear her heels against the floor. She's walking with purpose. She's probably taking it all in. My heart continues to race and then—she arrives.

Her goldie locks are strawberry blond now, thicker and longer than I remember. It's cut in layers, curly instead of straight. Her suit is navy blue with pink cuffs, pockets, and collar. Gold buttons keep her breasts from spilling out of the jacket—did she get them done? She gets onto the stand, and I get a good look at her face—beautiful as always. Her green eyes avoid me. I don't think we've ever looked each other in the eye before. And at this moment, I have to come to terms with the fact that she looks better than I ever have.

Her hand touches the Bible. "I swear to tell the truth and nothing but the truth."

"Thank you."

When she sits, my anxiety doesn't settle. I watch her, waiting for her eyes to fall onto me. But they don't. She doesn't even attempt to look in my direction. Do I not matter to her as much as she matters to me?

Has it always been this way?

"How are you today, Ms. Middleton?"

She hesitates slightly. She's not as prepared as Greyson pretended to be. "I'm okay . . ." Her tone is soft, delicate even. I'm sure she's perfectly happy.

Mara is also wearing blue today, except hers is more of a baby blue. Did they coordinate that? "And being just okay is perfectly fine, love."

Savannah nods. "Thank you."

"Savannah." Mara clears her throat and takes wide steps around the courtroom. "Would you be able to share your full name, age, and occupation with the court?"

"Savannah Middleton-King. But I do still go by Savannah Middleton, since that's the name I built my film and modeling career on. Oh, and I'm twenty-four."

"Thank you, and I see you have a ring there. Are you married?"

Savannah's gaze drops to the massive rock on her left finger. Another man proposed to her. Another man wants to spend the rest of his life with her. "Yes, to the father of my child." What the hell is it with this industry and early marriages?

"And for clarification, who are you married to?"

"Brandon King."

It takes everything out of me not to release an audible gasp. King. I should have known, and I definitely shouldn't have blocked her on every social media platform I could think of. How did I miss this? Wait—the father of her child. She was pregnant at the funeral. How long after that did Bailey and I break up? Come on, brain, work!

The timing doesn't matter. The fact remains the same. My sort of ex-girlfriend is her sister-in-law. Some-fucking-how. How does she keep doing that? Does she know? She has to know. Bailey has talked about me, right?

"Well, congratulations. That is a big step. Can I ask you, did you know Xavier Amari?"

She nods. "Yes, very well."

"And how might that have been?"

Savannah shrugs before a light smile shows up on her features. She shoves it back into a frown just as fast. She doesn't want to miss him, but I think she does. "We were friends, and then we dated for a while, got engaged for some time and then broke up."

Mara nods, knowing she's heard this all before but checking to see how the jury is digesting the information. "And how old were you when you met him?"

"Um . . . I was eleven. I hadn't known who he was then. But he and his nanny helped me in an incident."

"And what incident was that?"

She shifts in her seat, discomfort clearly shown by the way she's beginning to turn red. "I was walking home from school because my parents had forgotten to pick me up. I was attacked by some older boys, and they were driving by and took me to the hospital."

"I see. And how did you meet Xavier the second time?"

Evelyn stands and interrupts. "Your honor, relevance?"

Mara turns to her, her heat-curled hair flowing behind her. "I am getting there, your honor."

The judge nods. "Proceed."

"Mrs. Middleton."

"I was fourteen. Um . . . My mom was a pretty bad alcoholic by then, and I was just taking a walk. It wasn't safe of course." She scoffs. "But Xavier drove past me . . . I don't even think he had his license then." Her eyes fall to her lap, and an endearing grin appears as she tells the story. "But he stopped and asked if I needed a ride. I knew he looked familiar, but I couldn't pin from where. He was happier then, for sure. I told him no because I still went to the same school as him and everyone else in that district, but I actually lived outside of the, um, nice homes. In a small apartment because my mom got really bad with money after my dad left. So yeah, then."

"Wow, I'm so sorry you went through that. And then how did the rest of that relationship go? If you don't mind telling us the full progression?"

"Um, sure . . ." She clears her throat and takes a few moments to think before continuing. "We didn't start dating then. It was actually a year later. I didn't get close to anyone really, other than Jerrica because she knew that I didn't have the money I used to. We had a dance, and

Jerrica's dad took us dress shopping—he bought mine too. That's when she met Greyson—"

"Greyson Moore?"

"Correct. She started dating him. I got introduced to Xavier officially through them. Our first date was to go get milkshakes, and he made some joke about not being able to eat dairy. I thought he was allergic, but it was just his sports diet or whatever. Um . . . Things were normal, ya know? For a while."

Mara's eyes fill with sorrow because she knows what's coming. She has to. I'm sure whatever it is, she made sure to tell her to include it. "Go on, it's okay."

"My mom died, um . . . and I'm sorry, I know that's not what this is about, I just—"

"Take your time," the judge interjects.

Savannah sharply inhales and picks her head up to flash a forced smile. "I ended up living with the Amaris because even though Xavier and I were only friends, he couldn't fathom the idea of me having to move or being more of an orphan than I already was. And I guess that's how we started. His parents taught me everything: how to be a businesswoman, how to live on my own, and how to be a brand."

"And then what happened? How did high school end for you?"

"Xavier got pulled out."

What? I didn't know Xavier never graduated.

"Xavier . . . loved high school. He loved all the sports he played, the dances, the classes. And he was super smart too. I remember watching him toss everything out. He never wanted to drop out, but he knew that his future was in boxing. I tried to talk him out of it, but his dad was always a moving force in his life. That was the day I noticed he was doing steroids."

"So, you confirm that Xavier Amari was a drug user?"

"Yes."

"And how did he begin to behave due to them?"

Savannah shrugged. "He was more irritable, exercising all the time, really focused. But never wanted to be bothered."

"And did you see a change in his personality?"

"I did. But it was complicated. To me, he always tried to be the same. Sweet, amazing. But that doesn't speak on how he treated other people."

Mara nods. "Of course. So why did you break up?"

The woman gulps and pulls a piece of blond hair behind her ear. "We fought a lot with where to go next. He wanted a family. I wasn't too sure. He worked so much, and we were still really young. Then when we would break up, he'd get a new fling, but then he'd say it wasn't the same and we'd try again. Eventually, he couldn't wait anymore, and I just didn't feel right taking that step with him."

But I did. I'm the one who was willing to give him everything he wanted. Why did he even want her?

"Right, and do you know the defendant?"

"Yes. I know Arlissa."

Shit.

"Do you have a relationship with her?"

"I do not."

"And how do you know Ms. Benson?"

"I know she dated Xavier after me."

"And do you have any knowledge of any abuse between Mr. Amari and Ms. Benson?"

"I do not."

"Nothing further, Judge."

Evelyn stands and shoots a confident look in my direction. It's the first time she's ever done this, actually. She ties her small hands behind her back and heads to replace Mara's spot in front of Savannah. "Hello, Savannah."

"Hi."

"Very powerful story you have there. I do have a few questions. Is that okay?"

"Yes."

Evelyn smiles at both her and the jury. "So, Xavier is this caring person who gave you a home when your mother died. Is that correct?"

"Yes."

"And you admit that he has had foul behavior toward others over the years?"

"Yes." Tension builds in her shoulders, and irritation shows in the way she glares at Evelyn.

"So, is it possible that due to the trauma that brought you to him and the way he obviously treated others that he is abusive in his romantic relationships and you just didn't notice?"

"Judge, I object!" Mara shouts from her seat.

The judge nods and waves her away. "Relevance, Ms. Cyrus?"

"Savannah Middleton acts as a character witness to Xavier Amari's behavior. I am simply getting further clarification."

"Go on then."

"Savannah?"

Savannah gulps. "I am not here to speak on a relationship I wasn't in. And to be quite frank, I don't know what he did with anyone else. But I am very capable of knowing what is traumatic and what isn't. And the only thing that was traumatic was watching a boy who loved himself, his life, and the people around him turn into someone unrecognizable. Whether that was toward me or not doesn't make it any less true. But the fact of the matter is, that wasn't all I want to remember our relationship as. He wasn't a monster or a crazy person. But he very well could have been anything he wanted to be to anyone he chose. All I know is I hope what Arlissa experienced is her truth and nothing less, because he is dead, and he can't speak for himself. But I've moved on from him and her, and I will not theorize or speak on anything that is not my own experience. The Xavier I knew was kind and damaged, but who isn't? We all had things going on and made mistakes, and Arlissa—" She pauses to give herself time to look directly at me, homing in on my desperate need for her approval. "I hope you didn't. Because no one deserves to die. No one deserves to not wake up. And I can't justify that."

"Nothing further."

My chair feels like a spotlight now. I wish it didn't work out that way either, Savannah. For all of us. But I still love him, he's still my best friend, and I still hate him—I thought we had that in common. I thought you were just as dumb as I was.

FIFTEEN

*T*ruth be told, I didn't want to be seen after yesterday's court hearing. It didn't go bad, I don't think. But it wasn't a win either. Evelyn had nothing to say, and Madison didn't either. They all stared at me like they knew something I didn't want to know. But right now, I don't have the time to figure all of that out.

My gaze drops to my lock-screen image of Hope, the only thing I can focus on while the city streets move quickly on the outside of this cab. She hasn't even had a doctor's appointment, nor does she have any kind of paperwork. Is she sick? Is she crying? Does she miss me?

Failure fuels a variety of emotions. Shame, guilt, embarrassment, and anger to start. But it's even worse when you think you're doing your best—that's when it feels like drowning. In those moments, I made decisions that felt best for us. I refused to let Alejandra call an ambulance because I didn't want someone to catch a glimpse and put me on the forefront of every media outlet because Xavier Amari did in fact have a daughter. Now that I'm knee-deep in failure and guilt—I'll say it all out loud.

I don't think I want to die, but I wouldn't mind if I did.

"Here ya go." The taxi driver stops the van and presses a button to allow the door to slide open.

"Thank you," I mumble before jumping out with my head down and taking quick steps to the front door. My sunglasses are so tinted that I don't see anything in its right shade. My hair is straightened for once in a prideful attempt to throw people off. Today, I'm just another girl.

A taller man in a suit swings the door open for me and holds it. I nod to him silently and enter the air-conditioned building. The lobby isn't busy, but I don't have enough trust to take my glasses off yet. I make it to the front desk, and the woman looks up at me with a smile. Brunette, fresh lip injections; I can see a bit of bruising that she's trying to hide with a tinted ChapStick and some gloss.

"How can I help you?"

With every second that I stare at her, my mind takes me back to the first time I was in California. I was in an office similar to this with Aly. I was experiencing this same level of anxiety. The memory hits me like a ton of bricks, and for a brief second I'm unable to move or speak.

"Ma'am?"

"Hi." I shine an innocent smile and try my best not to rip my cuticles off of the bottom edge of my fingers. The pulsing in the back of my head begins to creep up. I push it away the best I can. "I'm here to speak to a . . . uh . . . One moment!" I quickly unlock my phone to gather the information I took down in my notes app. "Cata-Cata-lina Lang."

The woman nods and types a few things into her computer. Her gaze meets mine once again. "Yes! You're her one o'clock? Ms.—"

"Yes! Which way do I go?"

"Fourth floor." She points to the marble elevator door in the far right of the building.

"Thank you." I hike my bag over my shoulder and walk as fast as possible. I look to the floor as if I'm hungover, hoping the nightmares don't come now.

There was a time when going from my house to a van didn't include putting some pep in my step even if I was an hour early. Back then, I only prayed for elevators to be empty if I had to pass gas—not just to avoid small talk and awkward stares from people who recognize me but can't figure out from where. Those times made far more sense than the ones I'm currently in. If I could pass off my recognition to someone who actually wanted it, I would.

The elevator ding places me back in reality, and I step out. The fourth floor is bustling, with an open floor plan and different journalists and editors running around with earpieces and composition notebooks. I stand there awkwardly, praying my headache away and unsure if I should go in the direction of the closed offices or the group of people huddled together and sharing information. I should have asked what she looked like.

Somehow, I feel comfortable enough to remove my shades, so I do. In this room, everyone is focused on what they're doing, so invested in whatever story they're telling that a C-list celebrity standing in their office doesn't matter. Who am I kidding? This is probably their everyday life.

"Oh my god, hey!" The voice sounds strangely familiar, but I can't put my finger on it.

I turn to its direction and find a petite woman waving eagerly in front of a cracked-open office door. Her blond hair is shorter than I remember it, way more wavy too. Her Pink Floyd tee stuck out like a sore thumb when I was in that hospital bed, and wow—maybe I should have called that number.

"Nina . . ." I mutter and bounce my way over to her. "I guess . . . I should have known your full name. Small world." I clear my throat, hoping I don't sound as awkward and confused as I feel.

She rolls her eyes playfully and beckons me into the room. "No biggie! I saw your name, and I was like wow! What are the odds, right? I would have called, but I didn't know if you wanted me to. I know I came off kind of strong at the hospital, definitely not my intention. But hi! This is my office."

My feet carry me into the open space as slowly as possible. She shuts the door behind me. "So . . . You're a journalist?"

"You betcha!"

"And you didn't sell the story about finding me? That wasn't anywhere . . ."

She shrugs and takes a seat behind her desk. "I felt like that'd be a bit . . . unethical."

I raise a brow in suspicion. "You're an ethical journalist?"

"We all have lines that we say, *No, no, do not cross, Nina*! And that was one for me."

"Oh . . . Can I sit?" My eyes fall to the comfy brown

chair on the other side of her desk. It's practically calling my name since my legs feel like Jell-O.

"Go right on ahead! Do you like coffee? We have a pretty rockin' coffee machine."

"Nope, I'm okay. Thanks."

"Oh, come on! It makes caramel lattes."

"Fine."

Nina nods, stands, and pushes the chair back with her hamstrings. "I'll be right back!"

Before I can register her sentence, she's down the hall and has already turned a corner. I sink into the seat, allowing the feeling of uncertainty to soak into my skin. The AC roars above me, causing my eyes to wander upward and count the specs of gray spread across the white squares on the ceiling. I look at the vents and hope there isn't a bug waiting to splat on my forehead. My line of sight drops to her desk. It's neat. Nothing on it I'd expect a journalist to have, like articles or Sharpie markers. A single shut laptop, a "writer of the year" mug filled with gel pens, and a half-eaten everything bagel with jelly. Grape? Strawberry?

My eyes dart to a bottle of over-the-counter painkillers placed innocently on the corner of her desk. I quickly reach for it and unscrew the cap, dropping two pills into my mouth to dull the pain. First the headaches. Then the visions. Now I'm getting ahead of it. I briskly put the bottle back down and wait for her.

Nina bursts through the door. "I am a total ditz and forgot to ask how you like your coffee, so I made it as sweet as possible! I just kept adding sugar 'til it felt right! Shake, shake, shake, shake, you know? Just kept going 'til it was

Beyoncé colored!" A silly laugh falls out of her mouth like a rushing river and is only put to a halt by a snort.

I laugh too, hers proving to be contagious, and grab the cup. "Thanks."

"Of course. Okay! Let me be professional now." She places her own white coffee cup onto the desk and returns to her seat. "Hi."

I blow at the steam and place the cup in front of me. "Hello."

"How can I help ya? You called and said you had a story for us?"

The question is broad. I'm not sure where to start or really if I know myself. "Yes," I begin, but the rest of the sentence doesn't flow naturally. Where do you begin with telling a stranger everything you've kept a secret for so long? You don't. You keep your secrets, and then you die with them. I don't want to die with them. I don't want to go with a heart that heavy. "I guess I'll start by saying . . . I'm a mother who misses her daughter. And I have Amy Montana and Bruno Amari to blame for that."

The conversation pauses, although you can always argue that it wasn't much of a conversation to begin with. Truthfully, I don't know why I said that. Being that open wasn't why I made the call. It just happened. There's a discernible heaviness that sits between us. You'd think we were paying respects to the dead.

"Oh." Nina opens her desk drawer and pulls out a cell phone. After it's unlocked, a bright red circle pulses at the bottom of the screen. "Go on."

No.

I grab the device and press pause on the recording.

"If we do this, this is going to be the best story of your career—"

"You don't even know what stories I've done before, silly."

Our eyes exchange looks. "Correct. But I know my story, and I know it's the best damn story you can put out. But it won't be quick, and we won't be going over all of it today. And I need a few things from you."

Nina nods eagerly. "Okay, okay. Go on."

"Condition one, Hope doesn't get mentioned in any of this. I have my own way of dealing with that. But she does not exist to you."

"Hope's the baby?"

"Right. I was never pregnant. She has nothing to do with this story."

"It could make it more powerful . . ."

"It has enough material, trust me."

"Okay."

I hold my breath for a brief moment, hoping the words will string themselves together on their own. "Second, I need you to do research on a few people and let me know what you get back. And I need you to do your own research on my case."

"Why do I need to research your case?"

"Because I won't. I cut myself off from it all like nine months ago. Plus, I don't trust the information I've been getting."

Her pink lips part slightly but shut equally as fast. I can see her thoughts racing, possibly considering her options, wondering if I'm worth it. Truthfully? I'm not. I've messed up my entire life chasing rainbows with not a single pot of gold at the end. That's the thing about colors, they can be so misleading. You can follow the turquoise and end up with the blues. Chase the green and end up suffocated by greed. You can fall for a cherry-red touch but get scorched once it hits one hundred degrees. Everything pretty doesn't need to be yours.

"Deal. Who are the names?"

"Amy Montana and Evelyn Malik-Cyrus."

Chapter

SIXTEEN

*I*t was Nina's idea to start getting these interviews on camera. The last time I gave an interview was for a minor magazine that wasn't interested in my relationship with Xavier. That was rare. The camera lens is daunting. The black edges of it are eye level, but there's a kind of comfort in knowing that Nina is latching onto my every word. It feels like therapy, but I'm doing it for Hope. And maybe a little for myself.

"He made California feel like home. He showed me that love can be equally as powerful as pain. And I think when you come face-to-face with someone who can give you that much—you find everything else to be dull and lacking in color. I don't think people really get that. I don't think they get the fact that when the whole world looks black and white, you want to hold on to the one person who makes you see literally anything. Whether it's red or a different shade of gray—you start begging for the bare minimum. But when they start depriving you of that? When you start losing your goddamn mind at their hand? I guess . . . I guess that's when things get confusing. I don't know. You start wondering if it was them who made everything so bright and vibrant or just your want for them to."

Nina's ears soak up everything I say. "Do you need a break?"

"No, no. Let's keep going. I'm okay . . ." A pounding in the back of my head causes my eyes to lower. The sun is beaming violently into the office space. God, I wish she had some fucking blinds. I rub my temples casually and shake off the pain. I could use those pain meds right now, but I'm too scared to ask.

"You sure? You don't look too hot. And trust me! I know what it's like to not look too hot."

I shut my eyes briefly, and the grainy image of a room with no color returns. No one is crowding me this time. I look down to my arm, and the blue long-sleeve I put on this morning isn't there anymore. There are bandages. Why? I shake my head a few times, forcing the image out. My eyes open and then shut repeatedly until my blue sleeve returns—and so does Nina, and so does this office. "Um, yeah. Where were we?"

"You were going on about how great but also terrible things were."

"Right . . ." My train of thought leaves the station, and I find myself scanning my mind for a straw to grasp.

"We can take a break! Maybe get lunch and get out of this office. Wait, right. You said you can't really go out. Well, that sucks." Nina shrugs. "C'est la vie!"

My brow rises in confusion. "Huh?"

"You know! Such is life. That's life. C'est la vie! Shrug it off, water off a duck's back. That kind of thing." Nina talking too much but stopping at the right time makes me feel like a bitch for wanting to tell her to shut the hell up. But she's here to help. The only concern is whether she's capable of actually doing so.

Truthfully, this whole plan could go up in flames. I mean, I don't really have a plan in the first place. I'm digging an unmarked grave and hoping to hit a casket sometime soon, but there's no promise of that. I have to have faith. I can't think of another way to get Hope back and keep her from being seen as Xavier's property. I have to ruin Amy's ability to manipulate her die-hard fanbase. I need them to see me instead.

"Right . . ."

Nina leans in closer to me, and her blue eyes scan my body for a weak point, I'm sure. "Can I ask you something? On background?" To prove herself, she taps the pulsing red button on her phone to shut the recorder off.

"Sure."

"What are you so scared to admit? I mean, look at you, you're shaking. And I know that kind of shake, I used to do it. What are you hiding?" Her words are repeated by a deeper voice, but there's no one else here.

I blink frantically and forcefully rub my temples. I can't be that easy to read. There's no fucking way. But as I sit here in this trance where I feel comfortable saying things that I've never even thought, an answer arrives. "I've never been good at coping—dealing, I guess."

"What else?"

"Um . . . I never envisioned a life after twenty-four? Like, even with Xavier, every vision or dream that I had, I was still super young. And sometimes I wonder if me not being able to picture that means I won't make it that far. And since I'm so close to that age . . . I don't know. But lately, ever since I've had to go to bed without Hope crying or the worry of someone finding out about her—I want to make sure I make it that far. I've never felt that before."

"Go on . . ."

"Sometimes, I scare myself. Because I know the world could be on fire and my first thought would be wondering how Xavier is doing and hoping he's not burning up like the rest of us and then—" My lip beings to quiver, and the desk in my line of sight becomes a blurry vision. "And then I remember that he's not here. So, I guess that's fucking embarrassing. I still can't sleep on the left side of the bed, any bed! It's always his side. That's even if I can fall asleep in the first place. Sometimes I just blink, and it's the next day. I'm living my biggest fear of being alone. Which is wild because I've never hesitated to choose myself. I'm terrified that in the end, if worse comes to worst, I'll choose myself."

"I'm sorry . . ."

"I guess what I'm trying to say is I'd like to be my old self again. But then I also wouldn't? Because that self is so damn selfish. But she was also so ordinary that I hated her. Again, I don't know. I'm sure that sounds stupid."

The way her eyes sadden and she bites her lower lip, I know she pities me. The rainbow on her shirt catches my attention. I didn't notice it was there before. I look to the glass office door to the bustling journalists walking back and forth in their equally casual shirts. "When mine and Nico's grandma died . . . Things got really rough for us; mostly him, though. We lived with her because, um, our mom kind of sucked. But when Grandma died, we tried to drown it out, and Nico would go through these drunken phases where he'd quite literally dance through the house to her favorite music. And for a while, I assumed he was completely sane. But he's younger than me, so he was in a really fragile age range when she passed, ya know? Wasn't doing too hot. And one day, he just fell to the floor and said . . . 'Nina, I don't dance like I used to with Grandma, even when I close my eyes and pretend she's there.' And like . . . times like that you'd be like wow, this person is nuts!" She chuckles a bit, and I wipe my tears and follow her lead. "But grief is weird, and it messes your brain all up. It does weird things like makes you numb or makes you crazy. And then you have phantom moments . . . Find yourself clicking on their contact, maybe even letting it ring before you're like, gee! Forgot they won't answer! And Nico got out of it because, of course, he had me, and I'm pretty great if I do say so myself. But because he allowed himself to let it out. Let it out, girly! Let it go. Face the storms, if you will, because there's always a pretty little rainbow." She shamelessly points to the one on her shirt.

"Let go?"

"Just let go."

"Tha—" Words are cut off by an alarming ring coming from my cell phone. I quickly fish it out of my bag, and disgust washes over me for the first time when seeing the name Ellie appear across the screen. "I swore I told her to never—" I shut myself up and excuse myself from the chair. Nina nods in agreement, and I step outside of the room and find a less occupied space. "What?"

It's silent, but I can hear car engines in the background. Or a plane taking off?

"Hello?"

129

"Arlissa?"

"Why are you calling me?"

"Look, I just need to—"

"You let her take my child? *You* never wanted to talk?" I snap. Aly was right. She's always had a nerve about her.

She exhales. "I know what you've been saying about me."

"What are you talking about, Ellie?"

"Those stories, on the blogs. I know it was you!" I can hear her deeply inhale, and then her tone drops again. "Whatever. Amy wants to see you."

"Excuse—" Before I can get the words out, the line cuts off.

My blood begins to boil, and my heart rate quickens— why is Ellie so close to her that she's the one sending the message?

It'd be really nice to shoot the messenger right now.

Chapter

SEVENTEEN

Amy's massive amount of land doesn't look as vibrant as it did on my first arrival. That day, I drove up onto the property confused and unprepared. I swore the sky was covered by specs of gold. The grass was a vibrant green, and now there are brown patches all over the place. There used to be a bed of roses and lilies that dressed the property with a welcoming spirit that Amy simply doesn't possess. Now, the closer I get, the more muted-color petals I come across. The glowing orange lights aren't shining through the windows anymore. In fact, most of them are pitch black. The small house that was once mine and Aly's home has overgrown grass around the perimeter, and crows linger over the roof.

I should be excited about the possibility of being able to see Hope, I know that. But the truth is, I'm a silly little fear-based human. I stayed in my relationship out of fear of having to do everything over with someone else and the reboot being as lackluster as reboots usually are. I thought he was *Boy Meets World* and anything else would be *Girl Meets World* or worse—another *Saved by the Bell*. I latched onto drugs because I feared if I didn't mirror him, he wouldn't want me. I pushed a pull door for years and wondered why it wouldn't open.

I sink into my seat and park in the driveway. For a moment I wish the leather would swallow me whole. If things like that were possible, I wouldn't have to fear what I'm about to walk into. Maybe I should call her first and make my presence known because it's not like there's an element of surprise anyway. She's expecting me.

The door swings open before I can turn my headlights off to reveal a more wrinkle-faced woman than I remember. "Are you coming?" Amy shouts from the doorway, clasping her jacket closed with one hand and holding the door ajar using the other.

I scramble to pull my key out of the ignition and grab the red leather bag Xavier bought me to go with—the car. I miss that car.

I shut the door behind me and shake off any feelings of doubt that may have been left in the front seat. "What am I here for?" My voice echoes through the acres and startles the birds that were hidden in trees before I showed up.

"You are a very rude visitor. You are aware of that, right?"

I roll my eyes and head toward her. Anything could be in that house, but the promise of seeing Hope again keeps me placing one foot in front of the other. Amy steps to the side and allows me to enter, so I do that. The floors are as bright and spotless as I remember them. The golden atmosphere I recalled previously is no longer here, though. I can't be sure if it's me and my inability to see anything other than gray these days or if it's actually that dull in here.

"Where is she?"

Amy scoffs. "Who?"

My arms spread out in disbelief, and my face increases in temperature. "Who?"

The woman's veiny hands shut the door, and she takes a few steps around the open space where Xavier's achievements once hung. I wonder where they are now. "Let's say by some strange occurrence you clean up your act, you get out of this. Maybe get lucky with a mistrial." She stops herself and heads over to the kitchen.

I follow, remembering the floor plan of this first floor like it was my own. I've never been upstairs, though. I glance at the large staircase that leads to a dark hall. Is she up there?

"You manage to disappear like most Hollywood names who are too embarrassed and unmotivated to recreate themselves. Do you know why that is?"

I shake my head. Amy pours some red wine into a glass and brings it to her lips. Her gulp is long and inconvenient, like she's trying to prove something.

She smacks her red lips together. "It's because they don't want to deal with the initial hump, the initial embarrassment. They don't want to revisit the hell they just got out of. But you see, I have no desire to be humiliated. So I don't put myself in the spaces where humiliation can be created. You, my dear, you are different. You will follow people around like a dog in desperate need for water when a stream is right there, darlin'. Go! Go chase the stream, but no. You never see it even though it's right behind you.

Quiet as kept, that's a sad way to live. Don't you think so?" Her eyes sadden in a sarcastic fashion, only to be followed up by a smirk. "Which brings me to my question: What makes you think a child can change the fate you've given yourself? What was your plan, Arlissa?"

My hands form into fists, and her eyes immediately focus on that. "I am more than capable of taking care of her."

"Sure, sure. But are you capable of taking care of you? Because last I checked you're on trial for murder and my grandchild would have been—where again? With some woman who was never her family in the first place? You sure are one for putting the cart before the horse, huh?"

My bottom lip quivers, but I tuck it into my mouth in an attempt to hide my emotions. "I just want to see her."

"Ah!" She puts her wineglass down and wags her finger in my direction. "That is not what I had Ellie call you here for. Let's stay on track with today's agenda."

My posture stiffens with every vowel that comes out of her mouth. To think there was a time where I danced around my living room to her greatest hits. My voice strains. "So what is it?"

"There's been a plea deal offered. You would just have to say you're insane. Evelyn tells me you probably won't take it. As kind as I am, I thought I'd have a conversation with you. Come on, have a seat."

I can't wrap my head around why she's refusing to take off her light purple coat. I guess it's the same as not taking off your shoes in your own home when the person there isn't someone you trust. She moves through the space elegantly, allowing the garment to flow casually behind her.

"I'm not taking that plea."

"Because you didn't kill my son?" Her question ends with a sharp pause and a clear enunciation on the *n*.

I don't think she means that anymore. Did she ever? She sits on the powder-white couch, but I don't join her.

"Oh, doll, sure. Whatever you say, but this is the American justice system, and they have what we like to call evidence."

"It's circumstantial."

"But are you?" The blue in her eyes crystalizes, and if looks could kill, I'd be on the ground coughing up blood right now. In front of her is a beige folder, similar to the ones they held Xavier's crime scene photos in during my interrogation. This room feels similar—cold and moist. I'm dressed differently, of course. I don't have that white nightgown on, and there isn't dried blood stuffed under my nails. Yet I feel just as small, maybe smaller.

"Can I see her?" I whimper.

Amy pushes the envelope closer to me. "Take the plea."

My breath quickens, and every fiber of my being retracts as far as it can from that folder until I'm pressed against the soot-colored wall. My skin is soaked in fear. My blood boils momentarily but ends up taking a petrified pause. Weakened knees begin to tremble, and I rack my brain with the idea of taking a plea. "No."

"Take the plea. You can see your daughter sooner than you will if you don't."

"No! I'm not crazy!"

"Oh, of course not. Anyone who yells like that isn't out of their mind at all. Completely sound, all the way there. My son is dead, you know. The cause is less of the point to me compared to the fact of the matter being that he's no longer here. Do you think you lost something? You don't know half of what a mother feels. The longer this case goes on, the more pain you bring this family, when in fact there isn't enough evidence in the world to put me in your shoes. To make me understand why under your watch my son was just—gone. So sign it. Goddammit, sign the papers!"

"No."

"Then you are going to burn in hell."

If I can't see my daughter, there's no point in me being here. Why am I taking this? Why am I sitting here? I don't need her. I never did. "I'll see you there, then. I hope he saved us a fucking seat," I spit out. My feet carry me out of that house as fast as possible because being alone is safer than being stuck in four walls with her.

My quick breath carries me through throwing myself in the rental car and reversing as fast as possible. I run over a few dead flowers and only slow down to see the array of windows in my rearview mirror. Hope could be in any of those rooms. She could be waiting for me, and I'm too scared to make it happen.

In between heaving noises and my chest spiking up and sinking down, I make a few turns to a place only I know now. It's no longer an *us* thing. Everything that he showed me that became ours is only mine.

The cliff is still beautiful. Flowers that are in season bloom and spread a kaleidoscopic arrangement of colors. Blue, red, and brown birds stand out around the green leaves and greet me with a sound that's different from my own hyperventilation. I dig my phone out and press ten numbers that I know by heart.

It rings once, twice, three times.

Four.

Five.

"Hey, you've reached Xavier Amari. I can't make it to the phone right now, but if you'd leave your name and number, I'll be sure to get back to you."

A loud beep rings through my right ear. I wipe a fallen tear and sniffle obnoxiously. "I guess your mom still pays your bill. I don't even know where your phone is or if anyone has access to it . . . So, I don't know if this is a stupid idea or a good one. The only thing I know is that I need to talk. I've almost done this a million times, but I never—I never left a voicemail because I always thought that was pretty pitiful. Or I was scared, maybe? But Nina said I should let go, and the first step to letting go is coming to terms with the fact that you're never gonna answer. There's just so many times where I would run to you or Aly, but even though Aly agreed to be there to call when I needed her . . . I know she hates me. I know I'm not Savannah, and I guess it'd be easier if I was." I scoff and shake my head, tears wetting my jeans. "It's comical, really. She has a son that no one is using against her and Brandon—God, good job, Savannah. She has Aly now too. I guess you would have seen that coming. You were always really good at reading people. But she had you. I know you guys used to talk. I'm not dumb. Is that what you wanted? Someone more like her? I want to say you ruined me, but I think the truth of it all is . . . I ruined me. I just wish you were here to tell me how to fix it. Tell me how to fucking make this feel better! Because I try my hardest, and it never gets better. It just gets harder. Nina says it's life, but I think it's bullshit."

Beep.

"Your recording has reached the maximum amount of time allocated. To repeat your message, press one."

Chapter
EIGHTEEN

*I*t was a huge moment for me. I was hosting an award show, you know? That kind of thing would freak anyone out. Especially me. I'm not talented. I don't even think Aly has done that yet. But I was associated with the Amaris, so I got those kinds of perks. But, um, after a while I think Xavier got jealous? I didn't notice it then, but I think back on it now. He hadn't been asked to do it before either. Host an award show, that is. And faking sick . . . leaving early. I refused to believe it then, but he just didn't want to see me. He didn't want to support me. Like I said, I didn't notice it then. So I didn't do anything with it. I guess that's the problem with having a one-track mind. I was always in the moment, so much so that there were things that got away from me. Does that make any sense? I just looked up one day and had to deal with what happened the day before. I just kinda floated."

I turn my head before the sun can set. There are some things in this life that I don't want to remember how beautiful they are. I'm close. I've almost forgotten. I only look up or out of a window when it's gloomy and gray. It's easier to digest this way. I used to love the world and everything it offered or hid, I think. Or I just romanticize everything about my life before this year.

"I am telling the truth, okay! My hospital records . . . They don't exist. Um, the overdose, the car accident . . . I don't know. I don't fucking know. Evelyn said she looked but there was nothing in my name, and I can't tell you where they went. And the one person who knows? She won't go against Amy like that. I mean, come on. Look, I want her to be successful, so I won't say her name. But I hope that if she ever loved me, she'd know how important it was to back me up in this. To be my damn witness."

Five hours. Four coffee breaks. Three years' worth of stories. Two people. One camera.

"What is one thing you want the whole world to know?"

Mmm, good question. Can I answer? It's all about me anyway.

I shake off the thought, which is easier these days. He's not as loud, but it doesn't make him less present. "Um . . ."

Say something with a little sparkle to it, like . . . I want everyone to know that I am an amazing woman after all! His laugh echoes in my head. *No, no. We're trying not to lie, right? So tell the fucking truth.*

Tell the truth.

"If anyone is actually listening or watching or whatever, I hope they hear me when I say this: I suck." I scoff, rolling my eyes to the ceiling in revelation of the bitter truth. "I didn't offer Xavier anything, so who's to say I actually helped him? No one knows. I don't know. My stupid decisions don't make his any more valid, though. I was given a life I didn't understand, and I had cokeheads and bloodsuckers for mentors. I've lost everything. And I wish he could come from whatever urn they have him in and make this all go away—but he won't. Telling this story didn't make me feel any more like a victim. It made me feel responsible."

Hey, Sam. I did it. I gave you a story worth watching.

"I think we've got it," Nina says plainly while cutting off the camera and untwisting it off of the tall black tripod. "You okay?"

I become semi-present again as to where I am. The same large window, the same large office, except people aren't typing in their cubicles like the world is ending. I don't notice that my jaw is clenched, how my shoulders are at my earlobes, or that I've been gripping way too tight at my roots until I fully check back into my body.

"Lovely weather we're having . . . Would be a good day for the world to end."

"What?" Nina questions.

I blink feverishly and shake my head. Why did I just say that? It feels as if I'm conscious but not in control—like someone else is the administrator on my system. "I—I don't know. Sorry."

Nina slowly backs away as her bright pink nails grip onto the camera bag zipper to pull it open. She's wearing denim wash overalls and a muted pink shirt. Her hair is tied up in a white scrunchie that reminds me of when I was a kid. "Maybe you should—"

"How'd you get this office?"

The blonde tries extremely hard to mask the minor signs of offense off of her face, but a small amount still shines through even the brightest smile. "What do you mean?"

"I just—There's people here who are obviously older than you and look a lot more stressed than you, no offense. So how'd you get this office instead of them?"

"I work harder." She shrugs and avoids eye contact with me now. A tense silence fills the usually coffee-filled aroma, and I know when I'm not wanted anymore.

"Um, thank you. For all of this."

"Of course. And I'm still working on the research part. Some leads are just being tied up, ya know! A lot of people would rather speak on the backend, but as soon as I get all of that sorted, I'll let you know. This . . . this is going to be a really big story, trust me. But are you sure you want to do it while you're still on trial?"

I puff out my chest and try to mask the fact that I'm falling apart. "Of course. Um, can I ask you something before I go?"

"Sure."

"Have you met anyone like me? Someone going through something similar, I guess?"

She shakes her head. "No. This would be a first for me. But, uh, why?"

I sigh. "I just had a question about like . . . being in a high-stress situation. I've been having these dreams or nightmares that feel extremely real. And sometimes I lose track of time. Like I blink and I'm in another scene or something."

She squints, analyzing my every move. "How do you know you're not dreaming right now?"

"What?"

The woman laughs. "Kidding! Kidding. I'm sure it's just stress."

"Yeah, exactly what I thought." I push some hair out of my eyes and hesitantly gather my things. Her words echo in my mind as I process them. I guess I don't know. "Well, I'll see you soon. Call me if any of those leads come back."

Nina's eyes flash in approval as she waves me toward the door. "Yes, yes! Just give me a ring-a-ding-ding whenever you need to! Open-door policy, I promise."

The drive home is long, and when I allow my mind to drift off, I see people running away from flames and falling buildings. The world around me is crumbling, and the sky is nothing more than a digital dome that's peeling away bit by bit. I stop at red lights that I really want to run through. I look to my left to see a family loving each other between yielded left turns and see people on my right arguing with their partner about something I'm sure is miniscule. By the time I get to the porch that belongs to 3945 Miller Road, it seems darker. I know I'll be walking into an empty box with a roof. The truth of the matter is, no amount of decor or furniture can replace the sound of Hope crying. Or the moaning from Ellie when she's going through withdrawals because she insists on being sober when taking care of Hope.

My phone vibrates on my hip. I quickly take it out to read the name. Two missed calls from Ellie. How did I miss that? She can wait. I don't have the energy today. Control of my fingers is lost when the device slips through and hits the cold floor. I stare blankly and step over it.

The bedroom is pitch black, but I don't need lights to lie in the bed I've made for myself. I hate permanent things, and death is exactly that. You can't reverse it or go back from it. It's as if you've lost your sight or an arm. You can get prosthetics to make others feel better, but at the end of the day, you're still disabled. I am a reflection of what everyone has made me, and now that I'm alone, what am I projecting onto?

I hold the pillow Hope loved the most close to my chest, and the smell of formula smacks my senses. I close my eyes in hope for relief and release control of my mind and allow it to wander. I can pretend again like I usually do that I don't sleep alone. I can envision anyone here, and the comfort of what it'd feel like will appear.

Time escapes me, and a vision of myself in a khaki jumpsuit appears on the TV screen behind my closed eyes. I'm seated in a room alone with nothing but a bed and four walls. I look behind me to see a photo of Aly and me from high school taped to the wall. Next to it is a photo with my mother, father, and Samantha. We went to Disney World that summer. I haven't seen that photo in years. A woman walks past my room, and that's when I notice the locked door that keeps me from going anywhere.

My heart starts racing as the rest of the world around me begins to form. Brick walls, constant noise, but no one in this room but me. The heavy-set woman returns and pulls out a key to begin unlocking the glass door. "Come on, it's time for your medicine."

Fear immediately strikes me as I dodge to the nearest corner. I sink into the concrete between the bed and the photos and shake my head feverishly. "No. No. I don't want to take it. It makes me think crazy things!"

She enters my space with someone else now and begins to drag me to where I'm meant to go.

"No! I don't want to take it!"

It's only a nightmare.

Chapter
NINETEEN

ree branches scrape against the window and pull me out of a not-so-deep sleep. There isn't enough Nyquil on the planet to keep me asleep. There isn't enough sleep to randomize a different dream. How do I explain that when my eyes shut I see the same image over and over again? A tiring loop of dreary walls and good-for-you injections.

Sleep never used to come with a price. Now it seems as if I can't afford it. I tossed the covers off four or five times, but it isn't the heat that causes my discomfort. It's the fact that every time I close my eyes, I have the same dream. And every time I open them, I see the same shit. The same darkness. The same dresser. The same untouched side of the bed. The same flat-screen TV. The same air vent. The same emptiness.

My eyes flutter open when I fight myself awake. Once again, I'm staring at the dark space of my vacant bedroom. However, anything is better than seeing myself in that gray sweatsuit. I lie in bed and wish for a distraction—a reason to get out of the sheets and put an end to the pitiful attempts of pretending to sleep.

When I manage to pull myself off of the mattress, the bathroom mirror isn't any more forgiving. Dark circles sit under my almond-shaped brown eyes. Red patches find themselves occupying both of my sclerae. If I squint hard enough, the shadows in every corner of the room look like a version of myself that's more scared of its own reflection than the last. In the left top corner, standing in front of the bathroom cabinet, is a little girl trembling uncontrollably. She's trying to ignore the blood on her shirt in hopes that it's not really there. Her curly hair fits under a periwinkle winter hat, but the hat is slipping off little by little every single time she shakes. She's holding onto something—her sister's keys.

To my right stands a girl suffering from extreme heat damage. She doesn't smile unless she's in the presence of someone she loves, so she remains straight-faced. She bites her nails down to the cuticles and wears hoodies when she would rather skip class. Diagonal from her is a redheaded woman slathered in false confidence and designer coats. The woman keeps rubbing her nose in hopes no one will notice the white powder she's so dependent on. Does she know she'll give it up for a baby in a few months? She sticks her coke-filled nose up at every other version. And then there's me. A fragile me who hasn't eaten in what feels like days and who can't trust anyone at all. I grip tightly onto both ends of the sink and finally face the music. My curls are growing out, my lips are chapped, and my eyes can no longer open fully. I've failed.

Then Nina calls.

The emptiness of the building makes it clear it's Sunday. We still close the door, though. The air sings a different tune today. There was once a sense of hope in the clear air that's now replaced with a thick smog. You can cut the tension with a sharp pair of scissors, but nothing duller than that.

The large window shows a sky missing its main component—the sun. Scrapped pieces of paper fly across the window, and scattered leaves follow.

"Tell me you have something for me."

Nina can't decide whether she wants to smile or frown, so she alternates between the two. "I've got . . . a lot, to say the least. And I never say the least." The blonde pulls open her laptop and eagerly clicks the keys on the keyboard until the machine dings. "Well, firstly we can't run your story."

"What?"

Her mouth opens and shuts over and over again until she finally figures out what to say. "We can't run the flippin' story because Amy owns TCT. She bought it years before I started working here. She won't let a story about her release that she hasn't put her eyes on. All it'd do is hit the editors and come right back to my desk."

The sound of my heart breaking has to replicate shattering glass because that's all I can hear. "So it's over?"

"I'm not sure. But let me finish, and then you decide." She spins the computer around so that I can see the screen. It's an article detailing when Amy bought *The City Talks* and how it was the biggest news and gossip blog in the country during that year. "Amy Montana bought TCT when it was just getting its recognition, which is normal in the business world, right?"

"Right."

"Right! But during that same year, every single member of her family was basically paying their karmic dues. Amy had just gotten sued for failing to pay staff members on her Greatest Hits tour. Bruno was under fire because an old rumored mistress of his from the nineties had passed away from lung cancer, reminding everyone that she existed in the first place. Xavier was—"

I wince at his name, unsure why but it happens anyway. "Sorry, go on."

"He was in hot water for allegedly hitting some lingerie model in a Las Vegas nightclub. So I dug a little more. We've never released a bad story about the Amaris for as long as I've worked here, but it doesn't mean we haven't tried." Nina gets up and pulls some files out of her desk. A few black folders scatter across the reflective surface. "Open them! Go ahead."

I hesitantly reach for one and pull open the slick flap to reveal some printed papers that look like drafted articles. There's a few pen marks here and there, a question mark above the title of one, and bright yellow highlighter marks across some biased-sounding sentences. "What's this?"

Amy Montana's Ex-bodyguard Is Reportedly Seeking over $2 Million in Sexual Harassment Lawsuit.

Savannah Middleton Says Don't Deem Alleged Xavier Amari Victim as "Crazy."

Sources Close to Bruno Amari Says He's Been Trying to Divorce Wife Amy Montana.

"There are tons of articles that we have tried to push through with stories about her since she bought the company. The only time we were able to put any truth out about her was before she bought TCT. She's controlling the media, which made me—"

"Believe me?"

"Yeah. But that's not all. She owns our partner company, KCK Images. They're a paparazzi company that celebrities pretty much have on speed dial when they want to call them on themselves. Anything taken by or credited to KCK is an image they were called to take. You want the public upset because you're crying? Put on the waterworks outside of an Outback and call KCK to meet you there."

"Okay?"

She sighs, clearly annoyed with me not connecting the dots on my own. "Amy has tons of pictures taken by KCK. A bunch mostly from when Xavier died, and they're of her crying outside and making calls."

"You're joking..."

"I wish! But get this, it gets worse." She shuffles through the folders and pulls out one with a pink tab sticking out of the top. She flips open the folder and places it on top of the rest. There are some old magazine clippings, and they're all dated in the nineties. They're accompanied by some photos of Amy and Bruno before Botox and extreme hair loss. "There's an old story that a journalist at TCT was working on forever ago, and it was an affair between Bruno Amari and Pakistani model Nora Malik. Nora got all that publicity for essentially ruining Hollywood's golden couple, but then she just disappeared. There were rumors of her getting pregnant, leaving the country, a whole bunch of stuff. But I found these scrapped articles that were going to be printed and just never made it through. Nora decided to speak, and she wanted to speak to us." Nina shuffles through the papers before finding one in particular with a photo of a younger-looking woman holding a baby. The name Evelyn Malik is highlighted right under it.

"Wait . . ." I pull the paper closer to me and try my best to understand the writing on the wall.

"Evelyn is Bruno's first kid. Which makes her Xavier's sister. On top of that, her mother is the woman who died from lung cancer right before Amy bought our company. She's not some lawyer they hired because she has a good track record. She's Amy's stepdaughter."

My jaw drops, and a sharp stabbing sensation appears in the back of my head. This is supposed to be a moment of validation and redemption, but I just feel idiotic. A wave of nausea hits me like a ton of bricks, and the world around me begins to spin until I want to vomit. But yeah, I'm okay. I have to be. "You're joking . . ."

"No. But wait! It gets more interesting. I checked in with some underground journalists, the blind gossip of it all, if you will."

"Blind gossip?"

"The ones that post anonymous submissions and dirty things that no one claims they believe but they still read. They're the ones that call your favorite pop stars out for being cokeheads and the golden child of Hollywood for having anger issues or bad breath. Or they out your favorite toxic couple for getting a confidential marriage certificate."

"Okay . . ." My head continues to throb, but I attempt

to shake it off. Hope. I'm doing this for Hope.

"Anyway! So I did my digging! Evelyn is a celebrity lawyer, right? Which practically makes her a celebrity herself. There are some strong rumors that she uses her husband, Keagan Cyrus, to help her win her cases."

"What? What does he do?"

"He's an FBI agent."

I have to remember to close my own mouth. "He-he does what?"

Nina settles down finally and looks down at me. "He's an, uh, FBI agent."

"There was one when I got arrested . . . When Xavier died. There was a, uh, there was an FBI agent. And everyone told me I was crazy. Evelyn told me I was crazy. I told them I wasn't crazy. I said I wasn't. I-I said I wasn't. I kn-know what I said. I know." I lean into the chair, and the ground crumbles beneath me. I can see Nina's hands wrap around me, but I don't feel anything.

Everything is empty.

"I said . . . I kn-know. I know what I said. I'm n-not crazy. I'm not. I'm not. I'm not. I'm . . . I'm . . ."

How could something I should have seen coming become the death of me?

Chapter

TWENTY

I don't remember how I got home, but I remember waking up from what felt like the longest slumber in weeks.

Justification. I expected to feel better when someone validated my feelings. Except I'm still the same, with a little more knowledge. The truth was supposed to be my get-out-of-jail-free card. And it may still be that; it might still be what I've been looking for, but it doesn't feel any better. I don't feel any better.

I'm just a girl, and I think a lot of people forget that. I only wanted to fall in love and see the world. I didn't want to model. I mean, who really wants to do that? I wanted to live, and I did. For two years I lived. I wanted to know I was someone—someone good enough to keep. Someone who didn't have a devil on their shoulder telling them to push it to the edge until there wasn't anything to push anymore.

I am a girl who entertained an invisible crowd, because at the end of the day, no one really cared that much.

Frail hands grab the half-full bottle of Jameson and chug the liquid until the burning becomes too much for my throat to handle. Liquid falls from my chin and onto my bare chest. I sway on the mattress and allow myself to drink away every worry my untrustworthy head can conjure up. With half-open eyes, I rock myself back and forth and chug until the bottle is empty. My fingers release it, and within moments it gets lost in the blankets.

There's a silent song that the darkness I remain in sings; it tells me that I'm screwed. It tells me that nothing I see and no one I know can be trusted. It tells me that everything I dare to love will be taken from me one way or another. And in between the swelling chords and whimsical violins, it tells me that a life full of struggle isn't a life worth living at all. It screams, it shouts, it commands that I realize that I am no one. I am nothing but a speck in the wind.

Maybe I should burn it all to the fucking ground.

I sit up straight and sway to the song that reminds me court is in two days. Even though I chugged the liquid minutes ago, numbness continues to flow through every fiber of my being. It starts at the top of my head and then causes my shoulders to shimmy. It spends some time burning a hole through my chest and moves down to my ribs. They no longer feel like a steel cage guarding my organs from mass destruction; I don't feel them at all. It travels down to my toes, and everything feels like nothing as I get up on the mattress and dance between the layers of darkness. The shades allow some daylight to come through, but only enough to cue me on the time of day.

Did I always know that solitude fit me so well? If I did, I would have also known I was too crazy to love.

"You're not crazy, baby."

My eyes lazily open to the voice coming from the front of the bedroom. "I am . . ."

Bleached curls are frizzy from lack of product, but her brown eyes could cut through me if I let them. She stands before me wearing what could be either a purple or burgundy shirt and dark jeans. I look down from my stance on the bed at the woman I lost all those years ago. Brown skin is practically illuminated, reminding me of the furniture in this room that I refuse to see. The remote for the TV is on the floor in a corner and collecting dust. A pair of green sneakers Ellie left behind is sticking out from the open closet. But then there's her. The brightest thing here.

Samantha shakes her head and takes a step toward me. I back up in fear, but I can't take my eyes off of her. There's this pull to keep staring, to keep engaging. My mouth remains agape, and my eyes fight to stay open and focus on the spinning room around me. I drop to my knees in her presence. We're eye to eye now. But it's not frightening, nor is it illuminating. It's not anything at all. It just is. It's her.

"How long? How long are you going to refuse to see it?"

I shake my head feverishly. "See what? See what, Sam?"

"The truth. The truth in the colors, the photos, the headlines. There are clues all around you, and you haven't seen them yet. You need to snap out of it, Arlissa. You can snap out of it."

"No."

"Yes."

"I can't. No. I can't."

"You're not crazy, baby sis. You just can't let go. You need to let go. And . . . when you let go . . . you'll see it."

"I don't want to."

"Why not?"

I wipe the tears off of my cheek that's probably spotted with black mascara. "Because if I realize that this is all in my head, then I—then I lose you. I lose all of you." I stop myself once the word *all* slips off my tongue. I meant *both*, right? "I can't. No."

"What do you want to hear, Arlissa? What are you hoping to get from all of this?"

I shake my head as my throat closes and my mouth stops creating saliva. "That you'll come back. That you'll be here, and I won't have to go through . . . this! Because this is hell, and this is painful, and this is more than anyone should take."

"And that . . . that is the consequence of your actions, Lissa. Everything you've ever done has had an equally eventful reaction. It's the butterfly effect, baby. You cannot control or change your past, but you can give yourself a shot at the future. People die, people do bad things, and people make mistakes. That's just life. But you don't have to make it the end of yours. You need to wake up, Lissa. You just have to wake up!"

"No. No. No. No. I don't want to."

"This isn't right, Arlissa. You can't move forward like this. You have to acknowledge the truth. I need you to wake up."

"Huh?"

She points to the TV remote and steps out of the way so I can see the large screen that I haven't given power to in months. I didn't want to risk seeing myself on the screen by accident while trying to check the weather. My flaccid body stumbles off of the bed and somehow manages to get from one side of the room to the other. The remote flips around between my fingers for a few moments before drunken fingers can locate the power button. I hit it and strain my eyes as a bright light washes over the room.

"Good afternoon, Los Angeles. Before we check in with the traffic report today, we have some tragic incoming news. A few of our journalists are reporting live from a Calabasas household. Basketball player Nolan Johnson called 911 frantic after entering his home and finding his twenty-two-year-old girlfriend, Ellie Navarro, dead from what seems to be an overdose. This has not been confirmed yet. The prolific songstress was just days away from releasing her second punk-rock album with Carolina Records."

A photo of Ellie graces the screen, and I find myself gasping for air while my knees rub against the carpet. My heart beats out of my chest as helicopter footage of ambulances surrounding the mansion play on full volume. I can't make a sound. It's as if my vocal cords have been yanked out of my chest. Air fills my lungs but vanishes as quickly as it comes. My chest begins to get soaked in a rainfall of tears, and nothing makes sense anymore. Ellie, no. Ellie wasn't struggling. I would have seen if she was struggling. She would have told me.

"She tried to call you. She tried to talk to you, but you weren't there, Lissa. And I know it hurts, and I know you feel guilty, but you need to wake up. Just wake up."

So I do.

Chapter
TWENTY-ONE

"Did you have any dreams today?"

I think I'm shrugging, but I'm so drugged up that I haven't had full control of my body in what feels like years. It hasn't been years, though. I know that much. But if I've learned anything while being locked in here, it's that I can't trust anyone. I look down to the gray sleeves that fit perfectly around both of my wrists.

"Arlissa? Are you there?"

I nod. I can't remember the last time I spoke, but I barely remember being here. My mind often escapes to a place where I'm the hero, but as soon as I'm about to save the world, there's nothing. It goes away as fast as it came.

"Okay. I hear you've still been struggling to take your medicine. But you've been doing better. And you know what? They're thinking you may be okay to leave isolation soon. Isn't that exciting?"

I nod, but slower than the first time. My brain feels foggy. Maybe I'll be better if I take my medicine. That's what they all say. It feels good for a while. It allows me to dream and explore a world that's different from the colorless one I wake up to every day. In that world, my parents actually want to see me, but it's in my control whether they do or not. I can't tell you where they'd bury me when I die. I guess that's the consequence of disconnection.

I see them all in my dreams. I cry in my dreams, but it feels good and it isn't full of shame. I see Ellie. I didn't miss her call. We had a few more moments of girl talk and Chinese food, and I was there when she needed me. Until I couldn't be. I see Amy, and she's not a victim. She's a villain. And I conjure up my own sidekicks and future love interests, and there's a place for me. It's somewhere I can see everyone I love and create more people to share my heart with. There's a baby there who needs my protection—I have a baby. This dreamscape isn't magical and perfect, but it's a place that has light and is protected by a glass dome that only I can access.

But the glass has cracked.

"Good. Well, I'll see you tomorrow, and we'll work a little more, okay?"

I do nothing. She steps away before I can even recognize the fact that she's leaving. The woman leans over to a younger man that has been standing there the entire time—I think.

"We'll be changing her prescription. I believe I know something else that will help bring her back to us, make her more present, because we're not getting anywhere right now. And when we leave, I'll explain to you all about how we go through that process, okay?"

"Okay."

I don't know if she knows I can hear them. But I don't think she cares.

"We have to make sure she's a bit more responsive before transitioning her into the group."

The intern is listening, but his eyes are fixated on me. They're focused as if I'm the best science project he's ever laid eyes on. I mouth "hello" and he jumps. His eyes disconnect from mine, and his body turns to fully face the doctor. My gaze drops to my wrists, and before I can process it, she's gone and I'm being picked up by my left arm and escorted back to my personal hell.

Life slows down for a minute as I take each step before the other in my scuffed-up white sneakers. Other guards watch as this one drags me through the jail and to my box.

"Hey, Cyrus," they call out to him, and he waves, but we keep walking. He had a better job in my dreams. A better plot, a better outline. We all did. Ellie lived longer in my dreams. We got more time.

We get there faster than I remember us moving before. Yet nothing is fully accounted for in my head anymore. I flow with everything and allow life to take me by storm. A victim of a natural disaster is all I have been reduced to.

I counted one hundred and thirty-three steps before. I forgot to count this time around.

He uses one hand to unlock my room door, and every day he tells me the same thing.

"Maybe if you can learn how to play well with others you won't be here much longer."

I was scared at the beginning. I was scared the first time he tossed me in here like he's doing right now. I was scared the first time the large metal door shut and I was confined

to four walls that replicated my own coffin. But then I re-
alized that I'm better on my own. On my own I can close
my eyes and watch as Xavier grabs my hand and whispers,
"Come with me. Let me take you home."

We have the same date every night.

Chapter
TWENTY-TWO

One year ago.

*I*f you don't talk to us, then we'll have no other option but to believe you did it, Ms. Benson."

The man's voice goes in one ear and out the other. How can I comment on something I don't even remember? Thighs that haven't been moved in hours are glued to the seat at this point. Sweat and dried blood are proving to not be a suitable mix for my skin. I don't have anything to say anymore; in fact, I'm sure if I try to use my voice, nothing will come out. My vocal cords checked out on me hours ago. I checked out hours ago. At what point do you run out of tears? At what point does anxiety hit its peak and you come to terms with the fact that you're not dreaming?

I want to beg and plead for my sister to give me some sort of advice, but I think she evacuated when I found his body.

His body.

Cold, silent, and unresponsive. How can someone look me in the eyes and tell me I murdered him? How can someone look past the shock and not understand that my heart bled for this man for three whole fucking years? He pushed and pushed, shot himself up with syringes to keep me as far away as possible. I never budged. I'm the one who didn't run. I fought for our happiness. I watched him tolerate my existence until he felt like loving me again. I did that. All of that. And the thank-you I get is not only having to start over alone but also being told that I'm the one who did it. I sat through his nightmares, his drug binges, his disappearing acts, his fascination with other women—because I knew. I know he loves me. There is no way in hell or high heaven that he's gone. And in a few hours, this will all get cleared up and just be a case of bad press. I'm not the one who did it.

Was I the one? Did I do something I don't remember? Did I dream of the times he squeezed my shoulder too hard in public to signal me to shut my mouth? Did I then wake up, grab the closest sharp object I could find, and slice him open in his sleep? So deep that there was no way anyone could say it was self-inflicted? Up the stream to get the job done, across the pond for attention. I could have. I've thought about it. Like that one time at Greyson's birthday party when I walked outside looking for him and he was way too close to this blond woman. I wanted to kill him that night. Or the time where we swore we would finally get sober, and he spiked my drink as a "joke." I could have killed him then too. I was vomiting for hours. Maybe the time we lost the baby and instead of being there for me, he shoved my skull into a brick wall and refused to take me to the hospital. He deserved to die then.

But men are flawed, right? He's not entirely bad; he's an abuse victim. He just needs help—he needs me. I kept him on his feet, as best I could. And when it doesn't get any better than this, when the love doesn't get stronger—you don't just leave. You find other things to build on. He's my twin flame, the other half of me that somehow got separated in reincarnation. There won't be a day where I turn against him, especially not now.

"Ms. Benson, did you have any reason to attack your boyfriend?"

Yes. Plenty.

"Staying silent won't help your case."

But I have the right, don't I? Leave me alone.

No, I wouldn't have done it. There's no way I got up out of my sleep and did that to him. I didn't do any drugs last night, right? No. I didn't do it. He—no. I'm not saying that to myself because that's not what happened. Xavier was just as hopeful as I was. As I still am, as he still is. How crazy would it be to pray for a miracle right now?

Let's try again. Let's be happy again. Let's make a motherfucking baby. But he forgot to mention that a chapter in this story involves me waking up in the middle of the night and finding him soaked in his own blood. The metal, the chill, the cuffs that are finally removed from my bruised wrists. That's all I can remember. Xavier. Then this room. This frigid, damp, depressing room that's made to break the will of the already broken.

"Arlissa." Oh great, now the woman is talking. "I know how it feels to have a man beat on you. That's what you said he did, right? In your Instagram live? And I understand his ex-girlfriend is due in about three months. That's enough to make anyone upset. Especially if the baby is his."

I stopped shaking a few minutes ago, I think. The pit in my stomach isn't doing somersaults anymore. My heart quit racing, and my tearstained cheeks stopped burning. I'm numb. I only remember how this freezing room felt, but the truth is I stopped truly feeling it at least half an hour ago. Maybe when they brought me water, maybe when they showed me photos of his body. I couldn't even see where the slit of his wrist was. But maybe that's because of all the blood. How does a single person even bleed that much?

"He said he'd love you forever, I'm sure. They always do. It hurt, didn't it? When he didn't keep that promise? You were his girlfriend, and I'm sure he scared you when he behaved the way he did. You had no choice. You were just protecting yourself, Arlissa. And that's okay. If you talk to us, we can help you."

"Ms. Benson, we have reports that he told others you were the abuser. You took advantage of a stressed-out athlete. Covered his name with lies, and then you killed him. You insert yourself into a successful man's life and then destroy it. People like you are familiar with that pattern of behavior."

I'm going to rip my fucking hair out if this man says one more word. The woman too. Them and their "good cop, bad cop" routine can both burn in hell as far as I'm concerned.

I might not have much memory. I might not understand why I'm sitting here with cracked lips. I just know that I'm a black woman from Carson City, Nevada, who Xavier picked up and brought into his sparkling world. But not everything that glitters is gold. I never belonged, and now the outsider is being seen as a monster who sliced open the man she accused of abuse. Right? Is that what I'm being held for right now?

"Ms. Benson. You were the only one in that room. Your fingerprints are all over the blade we found next to his body. The cut wasn't done by Xavier himself. But it *was* done while he was knocked out on sleeping pills."

"Lissa, that's what your friends call you, right? I know they probably saw you suffer while with Xavier. I know they'd understand why you did what you did."

A spot in my head slowly pulses, creating waves of irritation as my brain fights to remember what happened last night. How did I get here?

I can't focus, squeezing my eyes shut in a desperate attempt to calm the rave in my head. My memories are begging, pleading for me to stop trying to piece them together—make sense of them.

I did it.

Oh God, please don't tell me I said that.

Oh God.

In the midst of this realization, I can sense everything again. I can feel the cold floor under my toes as the thumping of my heart against my rib cage announces itself. Just when I'm getting used to being dead inside, my emotions make a swift return. I don't want to keep remembering. I don't want to feel it. The tears flood my eyes like a tropical storm, and a wave of heat travels through my entire being—limb by limb.

"He's dead, Ms. Benson. Don't make this harder on his family than you already have by refusing to tell the truth." The male clears his throat before slowly opening the folder and revealing multiple bloody photos of the man I love.

"Look at these, Arlissa."

The man continues to lay the images down. My condo is now a crime scene. Yellow numbers scattered around the bedroom count up to a false solution.

"You were hurting. You had every right to be angry with him."

I miss the smell of Sea Breeze whenever he would climb into bed after washing his face.

"He loved you. He gave everything to you. Why'd you do it? He still had his entire life ahead of him."

If I close my eyes, maybe I'll get a chance to see him clearly again, see him differently than the last time.

"Arlissa, you seem like a sweet girl. It'd just be nice if you talked to us."

He's my best friend.

"He let you into his home, introduced you to his friends, his lifestyle. How did you sleep through that if someone else did it? Are you trying to convince us that someone else somehow made their way into your condo and assaulted your boyfriend?"

If he's gone, who do I have? I don't have anyone.

The tears continue to rush down, stinging my cheeks with every release. The organ in my chest beats with a rapid pulse, breaking every single time it hits flesh. I can feel it, every glass piece falling to the pit of my stomach while I desperately hug my body for an answer.

I can remember a few things, though. His smile shines brighter than the northern lights. His hair, when it's been a while since a cut, curls more toward the ends and sits on his eyebrows. There was a time before the entire thing we call love blew up in our faces. And we were celebrating the idea that I was pregnant . . . Yay. God, I fucking miss her. But . . . we went for a drive, and he wrapped his arms around me, and I smiled because for once he didn't smell like sweat or vodka. He smelled like vanilla, the refreshing scent of vanilla. And I just let myself melt into his embrace, the oranges and the reds of the sky dancing as the sun rose, and I knew right then that we were welcoming a new beginning. I just didn't know I was the only one who was going to make it through.

No one tells you when you fall in love that the person can just—die. They tell you, watch out! He might cheat! Watch out! He might forget Valentine's Day! And you get the rule book for those things, you get the how-to on how to deal with a cheater, a liar, a psychopath. Whether you choose to read that book from cover to cover is your choice. But no one tells you how to feel when you find your boyfriend dead in bed and before you know it the FBI—

"Why was there a man with an FBI jacket on at my house?"

They're stunned. I can tell because the woman that I'm looking at for the first time is trying to close her jaw. The man. Well, he clearly wants to spit in my face. For the first time, I'm looking at them. I'm dirty, my hair is frazzled, my nails are covered in blood, and I'm basically naked . . . semen-stained and naked. But at least I can finally look them in the eye.

At the same time, it's like something switched in my brain. A light bulb goes off, but instead of illuminating my insides, it starts a fire. I get ripped away from reality, and I know I'm physically here, but in my mind I see something brighter, something more worth it.

"There wasn't an FBI agent in your home, Ms. Benson. But I'm glad you're feeling up for a conversation now."

I want to be alone. I want to bask in the warmth of this

vision behind my eyelids where no one can bother me, and I want to live here forever. Pure isolation is the only place I can enjoy his touch. Put me away, I don't care. Just leave me alone. I've run out of fight. I've run out of patience. I only want to be left alone.

"I killed him." The words pour out before I can process them, and I don't break eye contact for a moment.

"Excuse me?" They both speak at the same time.

"I did it. And it was hard because I didn't want him to wake up, and I killed him. There. I did it."

The detective scrambles to get a fresh sheet of paper and slides it over to me. "Could you put that in writing?"

So I do.

"All rise." Lazily, I push myself up from the seat, eyes locking with the woman entering the space from her chambers. The room is draped in fifty shades of brown, the only pops of color coming from the court officer's uniform and the American flag. Her hair is down, and she looks younger than the judges I've seen on TV. My heart skips a beat with every step she takes. What does she know? What is she planning? Is she going to judge the fact that I look like I've been up all night? Because I have.

A lawyer whose name I don't care to learn is standing to my right. She looks full of herself and more excited to be here than anyone in this room. I want to be left alone. I tried to tell them that when they dragged me out of my cell. Some people just don't listen.

"You may be seated."

I can hear the shuffling coming from behind me. I don't know who showed up, and I don't want to turn around and see. It could be anyone. My parents, Aly, Xavier's parents. Ellie. Savannah. Maybe even Greyson. Every time a new name pops up in my head, my heart works a little harder. Not because it feels fear, no. I'm too disassociated for that. But I hope I at least look good. I'm going to be famous. I'm going to be on the front page of every news outlet all over the country.

"The United States vs. Benson."

If I close my eyes, she'll never begin talking. The trial will never start. Everyone will dissipate, and I'll be alone in a dark room with no one but my own arms to hold me. I'd rather have that. Or Christian. Or Xavier. Or the child I'll never have the chance to have. I'd take solitude and darkness before standing here with no way out. I'd take a bullet to the head.

I close my eyes and imagine myself in a suit, and my hair is cut and polished. I have lip gloss on, and I have someone who will love me enough to pay my bail.

"First-degree murder, because I understand there is no evidence indicating otherwise. Is that correct, Attorney Grant?"

The woman to my far-right stands. "Yes, Judge. As of right now, those are the charges unless there are any changes. We ask that the court deny bail for Ms. Benson due to the harsh reality of this crime, her mental state, and the risk to the late Amari's family, who have their own concerns about their safety."

"Evidence?"

"Ms. Benson confessed prior to arrest, and the arresting officers believe because of the nature of how they found her that she was under the influence of psychedelic drugs. She also provided a written confession that helped officials deem her mentally unfit to not only go back out into the world but probably to stand trial as well. On top of that, we have text messages from Mr. Amari's phone to his friends about how Ms. Benson frightened him, and he didn't trust her state of mind because of her insisting that she can hear her dead sister in her head. She is simply not well and should not be let out on bail."

"Do they believe that, or was there a drug test done on Ms. Benson?"

"Since this all occurred only a few hours prior, it is only speculation."

"How is that an excuse to not get a drug test done on who you suspect if that was a part of your argument, Ms. Grant?"

"I understand."

"Defense for Ms. Benson."

"Your honor, the evidence presented against my client won't survive a hearing as you previously pointed out. The confession was before my client was given her Miranda rights. So I motion to have that initial 'confession' thrown out. As for the second, she wrote down: 'I killed him. Now take me away,' after hours of hassling from detectives. I still believe a psych evaluation would be useful prior to trial. And she was not on drugs. She was in shock due to what we all know she woke up to."

"Your Honor, we have other evidence."

The woman opens a laptop, and suddenly the giant screen next to the judge lights up. It's Xavier. I immediately recognize the interview. It's the same one that played when I watched him slander me on live television. Wow, he looked so good that day.

"Here we have a video of Mr. Amari, a few weeks before

his attack, speaking on the toxic nature of his relationship with Ms. Benson. If you zoom in on this shot here, he has scratches on his hands."

My lawyer scoffs. "He was an athlete. This video does not prove that my client is the violent one. If anything, it further proves that Mr. Amari simply has a profession that results in physical wounds."

The judge doesn't say a word, and if this were a movie, there'd be some grand orchestral fanfare playing in the background to signal my sudden doom. You can hear a pin fall in this courtroom, as if everyone stopped breathing. I sit here, resisting every urge to bite my nails.

"I understand." The judge finally speaks, sitting up taller in her seat. "Are there any additional arguments?"

"No."

"All right."

Silence.

I glance around the room, waiting for that push, and then it comes. I lean over the table and allow my elbows to hit the other edge. "I'd like to say something."

Audible gasps travel throughout the room. I ignore them. Panic washes over my lawyer as she stumbles to figure out where this is going.

"Go on."

A tired smile creeps along my features. "I'm fucking losing it." A rhythmic wave of laughter follows after the sentence. Half of it comes from the embarrassment of wondering what the fuck just came out of my mouth, but the other half from the rush of actually saying it.

Mumbles and disgruntled tones fill the air as I slide back into my seat.

"Order. Order," the judge calmly says while hitting

the gavel down repeatedly. The sound silences them, but it doesn't take their eyes off of me. I can't see them. I choose not to. But the burning at the back of my neck has yet to go anywhere. "Thank you, I will give my ruling then."

This is it, Arlissa.

My God, she's here.

It's home or it's jail until God knows when.

"I'm denying bail for Ms. Benson. Instead, she will be placed at Melron State Hospital indefinitely under the grounds of insanity. Thank you."

"No! She needs to be in jail!"

I stumble out of my seat and turn to see where the voice that's shouting behind me is coming from.

"She needs to be in jail!"

Willow? I haven't seen her in so long. At least not since I embarrassed myself and accused her of wanting to be with Xavier. My gaydar wasn't working very well then. Her curly brown hair is now straight and cut to her shoulders. She also looks like she hasn't had a full night's rest in a long time.

"She killed him! She fucking killed him! How are you just letting her go to some hospital?"

"Order! Order!"

"Get her out of here!" my lawyer shouts.

I gulp, watching people scatter around me.

"She killed Xavier! She needs to be rotting in prison. Give her the death sentence if you have to!"

"Ma'am, if you continue, I will have to hold you for contempt of court. Officer, take her outside."

Willow continues to point in my direction, fire-fueled tears dripping down her cheeks as the cop drags her out the door. She's kicking, screaming, cursing. But I don't blame her. I can't blame her. Because I'd be behaving the same way.

"She needs what happened to him times fucking ten! Does justice not matter to you people?"

"Order, order in the court."

I'm frozen in fear, unsure of where to go from here. My entire body numbs all over again, the only thing keeping me from collapsing right now being my sheer inability to move. I scan the audience. Everyone has their eyes on me. Everyone can see how petrified I am.

I shake my head and squeeze my eyes shut. I try to imagine anything but this. Maybe a world where anxiety that's this crippling doesn't exist. If I can go there, I don't have to be here.

Chapter
TWENTY-THREE

Now (for real this time).

*H*ey, wake up. Are you with me? We've changed your medicine in hopes that this will help you do better, okay? Help you be more present and with us."

The assistant doctor hovers over me.

Wake up. Wake up. Wake up.

It repeats like a symphony. A call that whispers from the trees whose branches act as an invisibility cloak. Sometimes I catch a glimpse of the lanterns that glow and fly toward the sky when a patient dies. It's a weird tradition here. You'd think they care.

The day I was thrown in here, I was never promised a day of getting out. Maybe that's the mercy of people who spend their years held up in a jail cell instead. They're trusted more than those deemed insane, which I think is a bit backward. The people in Melron State Hospital are seen as dangers to society because their brains function differently. Which is utter bullshit, by the way. How is it that those who are in their right mind when they commit the acts they do aren't seen as more of a threat? They have to be. They're the ones who can differentiate right from wrong, reality from delusion. They have a moral compass. They're the ones who should be taking medicine to get their brain right. Some of us have been living in a dream state to avoid coming to terms with the fact that time has been passing without us.

I tried, I did. I tried to check back in when Ellie died. But the way that news was delivered to me was different—harmful even. The prissy lady who gives me my medicine told me, but in a way to get me to speak. It's a running joke around here. Arlissa, the girl who killed the boxer, hasn't said a word since she got here. They thought injecting me with whatever shit they were using would make the game more fun, see which doctor I finally muttered a royal "fuck you" to. What they didn't know was that it was only making my dreams more immersive—more real.

Before I created an elaborate vision that I could easily close my eyes and experience—I was scared. Instead of screaming, I'd fall into a meditation-like state where the straitjacket no longer carried any weight. I didn't smell the vomit of the guy who pukes all the fucking time anymore; instead it just smelled like Northern California. The colors were brighter, and a glass dome was built around every scenario to protect me from intruders. I was staring at empty stars and creating false starts. I was building landmarks in my mind, and I felt it all. How could anyone tell me that's not real?

I remember trembling, and the night sky would look down at me and command me to do something about it.

I'd go from crying and throwing up about everything life has become, to focusing on a movie screen where I'm the star—right in the center of the frame. Although, the credits rolled a bit early.

Delusional. Hallucinating. Silent. The words are all thrown in my direction, and they never miss no matter the distance. The human mind is a funny thing, really. Mine is, at least. Anyone else fails to deliver the punchline, I suppose. See! I made a joke.

In my government class in high school, I learned that those deemed criminally insane aren't actually criminals at all. How could they be? They've been cast away to a hospital because they're technically not responsible.

I don't think I'm crazy at all, and I definitely don't belong here. And even though I haven't said a word to anyone here, I know it's not what everyone says it is. The people here can hold a job, whether that's hosting team yoga or mopping up after lunch. They're smart and articulate and have the same needs and wants as people outside of the ten-foot-tall gate. We, not they. We're smart. We're articulate. We have a pool.

Look, new conscious self, I'll take you around. I'll prove it to you! I'll even talk to them to prove it to you! Or to me. Or to us.

There's a lot of waiting around during breakfast. It smells like oatmeal and stevia, and there's always an annoying draft. They told me I have an option of wearing something else other than this gray sweatsuit, but it's the only article of clothing I can imagine myself feeling comfortable in.

A woman hands me a spoon and bowl of already portioned nothingness. I eat slowly in hopes that I won't be dragged to the next occasion. But when time is up, time is up. There's a guy to my far right who is playing chess and a girl to my left who is squinting at the small TV on the other side of the room. I don't waste too much time staring at them. I continue to chew slowly. There's a nurse hovering over me. I know what she's here for, and it's annoying how she lingers and waits until I've chewed just enough.

"Here is your medicine for the day." The nurse places the pills on the steel table, and when she bends, I can see her name tag: Evelyn. My eyes travel up to her features to see if she resembles the one I've created in my dreams. No. This one has stringy hair and a botched blue dye job. Her skin isn't as golden, and her eyes droop in a way that she should honestly get fixed. There are two honey-colored tablets that are different from the white ones they've attempted to shove down my throat time after time. The white ones came along with an oval-shaped multicolored one, something that looked like my mom's B12 vitamins, and a circle one with rainbow specs.

Everyone else gets up and goes to group therapy. Well, everyone who has earned that right. I know where I go after this—my room. I sigh and stuff the new medication in my mouth, chasing it down with a nice big gulp of room-temperature water.

"Wow, I'll be sure to tell Dr. Fletcher how easy it was to get you to take your medicine today. Good job, Arlissa."

I don't say a word in response; instead, I get up and prepare for them to take me back.

Everyone else has already fled the scene, heading to their therapy sessions where they practically hold hands and write in journals. They don't care that I'm a celebrity, or was. Half of them don't even know, they've been locked in here so long. I'm just a girl. The girl who wears her hair in two braids and doesn't say a word. I guess that's my narrative to change. Which would make it my job to change it. I would, you know. If there was a reason to fight for this life like I fought for the one they said was in my head. How can I prove that? What if this is in my head?

"We won't be going to your room today."

I look up at the woman, confused.

"You have a visitor. Follow me."

That almost provokes an audible gasp from me. But instead I follow her silently and pull my oversized sleeves down to cover my trembling hands. She pulls open the glass door where security stands idly by, and my jaw drops at the sight of the person at the other end of the table.

She looks great. She always did, though. Even when the other patients turn on the TV to watch some morning talk show and she's dripping in rubies on my television. I have to act like I don't know her and like it doesn't hurt. I guess that's the strangest part of this whole experience. Someone I used to share a bed with on weekends and sneak out with on weekdays is now someone I have to slowly creep out of a room to avoid spilling out the disgusting words: "I used to know her." It's embarrassing. However, what's more embarrassing is having to explain why it's in past tense. So I don't.

"Aly?"

Chapter
TWENTY-FOUR

The enticing thing about delusions is that they stem from truth.

It's true, Aly doesn't talk to me anymore. But the reason is not so easily explained as me sleeping with Christian. Which I honestly don't even think she knows about. Even if she did by some possibility, it doesn't even matter anymore. The reason is because she ghosted me. I understand she was put in a compromising position, trust me! Honestly? I wouldn't have talked to me either.

Holly dumped me via public announcement with a lengthy Instagram notes app message about domestic violence and choosing peace. How do I know? My lovely therapist printed out a screenshot in a desperate attempt to get me to talk to her during week three or something. I cried in the bathroom after and realized the meaning of the word *indefinitely*.

I want to pinch her, see if it's really her this time. But truly no one knows better than me how pointless that is now. My dreams felt real. No, they were real, real enough to get me through.

"Hey."

Her bangs sit an inch over her eyebrows. I always hated that style, and she always told me she'd do it one day because it's *so Vogue*. The rest of her hair that hasn't been cut in the worst style ever is straightened and tucked back behind her ears. Wow, it's gotten so long. An "AGM" necklace hangs from her neck. It's not coated in diamonds, just a modest silver chain that probably doesn't rust in the shower. Good for her. Thick eyeliner perfectly accentuates her siren eyes, and contour brings out her square face but also those killer cheekbones. I have never wanted to be her more than in this moment.

"Hi." My voice cracks at my first attempt to speak in months as I scramble to pull some scattered pieces of hair behind my ear. You can't erase months of not taking care of yourself in a single moment. There will always be a trace of the forgotten care somewhere, because how can you remember something you decided to quit? Overgrown toenails, unkempt eyebrows, jagged fingernails, and split ends just to name a few. Not that I've stared at myself in the mirror recently, but some things you simply know.

When I sit down, she leans back. Then shifts to the right. Then back to the center. Lack of trust. Never experienced that with her before. She fidgets with her perfectly manicured nails yet continues to be a flawless representation of how the outside world is still moving on without me, spinning on an eternal axis, and I'm stuck in here.

"How have you, um . . ." She clears her throat. "Been?"

I watch as her eyes shift from the guards back to me. It's hurtful, really. She doesn't even know how much it means to me that I am spending my first conversation token on her.

"Um . . ." My voice remains horse, but I clear my throat a few times and hope that it helps. "Well. I'm here."

Aly gulps and presses her nude matte lips together. "Uh, true! But I . . . I don't know. I guess—"

"You assumed I'd be getting—"

"Help."

"Used to things?"

She raises her shoulders and lowers her chin, but the silence in between the movements only makes things worse. "Yeah."

I shrug. "I don't . . . I don't, uh." My new medication must be kicking in because I go from focusing on her to only seeing an out-of-focus blob of a person. I hold my eyes closed for a moment and open them again. The action repeats until she's somewhat clear again. "Why are you here?"

Aly's mouth opens and then shuts immediately. She begins pulling on a stray string of fabric hanging from the bottom of her black off-the-shoulder blouse. "Honestly? Your doctor called. They wanted to see if I could help get you to . . . uh, adjust."

"She could have called literally anyone else."

She rolls her eyes, and all signs of sympathy melt out of her system by the time I put a period at the end of my sentence. "Fine. Be a bitch. But you're talking, so it worked."

"I'm talking because I'm confused as fuck," I reply in a nonchalant tone.

"What is there to be confused about?"

"Why you're here for starters."

"I just answered that fucking question." Her Latin accent comes spilling into the conversation, only annoying me more.

"No, that's not a good enough answer. Your best friend is being drugged so badly she can't even tie her own shoes for God knows how long because I refuse to look at a calendar or anything that can make me come to terms with this, and you're—you are nowhere to be found."

"What was I supposed to do?"

"Not abandon me in the situation you helped put me in."

The guard flinches, so I sink into my seat to show that I'm not the threat here.

"¿Qué coño?"

"Dude, I—I don't know what you're saying." My eyes hang low, and I try my best to take her seriously, but I can't.

"I helped put you in here? You're joking, right?" the woman spits out. Alejandra leans forward, which makes this the closest I've been to her in a year, maybe. "I didn't make you kill him."

I lean forward as well, lowering my tone in order to match hers. "And I didn't kill him."

Her eyebrows remain stitched together as she scoots her seat back—I've made her uncomfortable. "You can lie to anyone else, but you can't lie to me. I know what he did to you. I was there."

"So why did you let it happen?"

She says nothing and doesn't do anything either. It makes me feel like my question has stopped time, and now we're both sitting here in silence. I guess I'll break it.

"The difference between you and I is that I don't pretend to save everyone. So what if I saved myself? I'm so fucking fine with that. But you? You pretend when it's convenient. Because if you really cared, you wouldn't have showed up like it was a damn meet and greet."

She exhales sharply and scoffs. Her hands then press against the table as she lifts herself up to leave her seat. "You know what? Fine. I tried. But you murdered my husband's best friend. No amount of smart comments can help you run from that, Arlissa. I hope you know that."

What do you think you'd be capable of if you decided to take control of your life, Arlissa? I am genuinely curious as to what your answer might be, because being able to avoid reality and live in your head for as long as you have is a talent. But it's also a defense mechanism. And now that we've broken that wall—what now?"

I roll my eyes and try my best to focus on what she's saying, but the medication makes me so dizzy that if I look at anything but the black pen attached to her jacket, I might get carsick. And if we're being real here, I don't want to pay attention. The venom that spewed out of Aly's mouth wounded my ego in ways I can't put into words. When it's other people, it's fine. When it's strangers, it's whatever. But when it's someone I went to prom with, it makes me wonder what I ever did to deserve losing everyone I ever said "I love you" to.

"Aly?" It echoes in the back of my mind.

"Huh?" Can she read minds too?

"I said, Arlissa, are you listening?" Oh, no. I'm just hearing things again.

"Oh, yeah. Yeah. I'm listening."

Today we're using the same room they perform group therapy in. I guess it's some lame attempt to show me what I've been missing. The idea is that light brown walls and forest-green chairs are supposed to pull a fun case of FOMO out of me or something. It doesn't.

I curl up onto the padded seat and chew on my cuticles until they bleed. There's a strong smell of bleach in the air that makes my nose sting. Her white scrubs make her ginger tresses stick out more. I remember having red hair. Why does she hide it in that messy bun with that hideous black headband?

"Was I supposed to answer that?" I inquire before spitting out a chewed-up piece of skin onto the scratched-up floors.

She sighs and pushes her glasses against the bridge of her nose. They slip a lot. I don't know if she's too broke to get glasses that fit or what, but it's annoying. "I think you overanalyze. I think you obsess and become consumed with your own thoughts. Or some days you could avoid going down the terrifying wormhole of thinking. You're scared of that, scared that you'll lose everything or—yourself."

My nod delivers with a bit of tightness to it while I desperately try to hold my tongue. "Did you get all that from me just speaking today?"

"No. Patterns, human behavior, history. It's all very telling."

"You don't know me or my history," I point out.

"Arguable. I have court documents. Articles on top of articles, tracing your every moment from the day you moved from Carson City to California. I know that you're terrified you'll be stuck here forever like anyone would, and I know you thought you experienced your one great love. But most importantly, I know you don't think you have much to look forward to anymore."

I roll my eyes. "Sure."

She shrugs, and a few ginger strands escape her messy bun. Her long fingers grab her pen and begin scribbling on the notepad. Stupid, irrelevant notepad. She has a recorder. I can see it. It doesn't pulse as brightly as the one in my dreams, but it still counts for something. "You have a very interesting case here, Arlissa."

"And what is my case, Nancy Drew?"

She presses her lips together in disapproval. "There are other factors that need to be taken into account here, like the entire spectrum of human emotion. For example, mourning the loss of a child can cause intense changes to a person's mental state."

I freeze and wonder how much of my dream fuel was common knowledge. "Interesting," I tell her, pretending that last sentence didn't strike a nerve. "And what's that? The, uh . . . human emotion thing?"

"Anger, sadness, joy, fear, and love. But those are just five out of eight of the primary emotions. You see, the primary eight can be broken up into five more, and those five can be broken up into another ten or eleven. At this point things get complicated, and they blend into each other. For example, the feeling of agony can blend into both sadness and anger. Feeling jubilant can blend into both love and joy. I don't think human emotion in its entirety or its full power was ever taken into account for you, Arlissa. I don't think you're crazy or any of the other labels the medicine you take is proven to treat. I think you feel too much. So much so that because you spent so much time suppressing it, you never learned how to work with it. And working against it has . . . brought you here. But you know what I think?"

"I'm sure you'll tell me anyway."

"I think you just want to experience love again—in any form. But the only place you've learned how to both control it and experience it is in your own head. And that's where you hide everyone and everything you want to keep. In your head."

I hear the words, but they don't fully register. The entire spectrum of human emotions is bullshit. People have bad days, and they stub their toe. People have good days, and they get an ice cream sandwich before bed. People don't have bad days and just murder someone unless they're out of their fucking mind. I'm batshit crazy, and that is so much more comforting than blaming it on a bad fucking day.

"Yeah, okay." I roll my eyes and sink deeper into the chair.

She turns the recorder off in a painfully slow manner. "Do you want to be diagnosed with something, Arlissa?"

"Does anyone?"

"I'm asking if you do."

I cringe when our eyes meet and sink as deep into my chair as my body will go. "I just think there has to be a reason for my dreams . . . For everything."

She sits up, and her eyes flicker for a moment like I'm some kind of prized horse. A code she just cracked or something. It makes the hairs on my arm stand up, but I rub them back down.

"A lot of the time, we find ourselves falling victim to someone else's story, so much so that we forget our own. But—"

"Let me guess, 'You know what I think?'" I mock.

Theodora leans forward. Did I forget to mention that? Yeah, the nosey, know-it-all doctor has a name. "I think that's what happened here. You're playing crazy because you feel you're supposed to be seen as crazy. But I don't think you are. In fact, I think you play crazy quite poorly, if I'm being honest. But of course, you can let them label you as whatever they want and share a home forever with the twenty-four-year-old that slaughtered his parents and four siblings in broad daylight. Or you can talk to me. Talk to me and let me help you. Your story is fascinating, Arlissa Benson. It doesn't have to end here."

I lean forward because for once this makes sense. She's right. I could get used to the pool and eating everything with a spoon. I could talk to the twenty-four-year-old she's speaking of and maybe have some sort of relationship. Everyone knows him. Even in my drugged-out, half-awake state, I know of him.

"How? I mean . . . What do you mean?"

She continues to lean forward, so much so that our noses are aligned. Hers is more pointed than mine, definitely longer; I focus on the nostrils for longer than what's deemed polite. "I mean I want to help. Let me help."

"Not until you tell me how."

"Do you want to get out of here one day? Maybe even sooner than later?"

"Obviously."

"I can help you do that."

"So help."

A sly smile forms from cheek to cheek and showcases a small dimple only on her right side. "Good. We'll talk tomorrow." Her attention falls back down to the red recorder button, and she presses it so that it can begin again. The timer starts back up, and the white digital numbers start changing at their normal millisecond to second to minute speed. "So, how are you feeling?"

She smiles at me.

"Terrible."

I'm confined to a room at the edge of the large building. It's not-so-nicely decorated, with peeling paint on the gray walls and a single bed placed in the middle. My two pictures remain taped to the wall. I don't know how they got there, but I guess you miss a lot when you're drugged and on another planet. And that's why I need to get out of here.

I can only assume Theodora wants me to participate, talk some more. Maybe I can talk my way into an appeal. I didn't get any details, but I guess that being a model patient is the only way I can get out, right? Nothing else would make sense.

I rip the pictures down from the wall, starting with the one that Aly's in. She looks so happy. But she'll never smile that big next to me again. I want to rip them up into tiny pieces. What if I forget what my old life looks like?

Theodora is right. I'm not insane; I was grieving. Shit, I'm still grieving. Even though this isn't prison, I wonder if it's worse.

In prison, I could have missed a meal. In prison, I could have stayed in my room all day and mourned one of my best friends. In prison, I'd have the choice to sit in silence—maybe even in the hole—and watch my demons take me through the motions of loss and destruction. If I was in prison everything I did would be a choice, not another word on the growing list of symptoms. At least that's what I've heard.

I plop down onto the bed and stuff the pictures under my single flat pillow. I stare at the glass door that keeps my eye on the hall and their eyes on me. I could spend my time napping, but instead I stare. I can't afford to fall asleep now, especially since I have no idea what they've been shoving down my throat. If I sleep, I can't promise myself I'll wake up in this world. I need to be present. I can't sleep.

My body jolts up to the sound of keys coming down the hall. It's followed by footsteps that give off an echo of large heavy boots. It's probably the black ones that all the guards wear. But behind those are significantly lighter steps. "What do you need, Tyler?"

Tyler?

"Arthur! Just the guy I was looking for. We were having group yoga, as we usually do, and Michael just vomited all over the place. He needs some help. I think he's seizing or something, I don't know."

Oh, that's the massacre boy's name. I recognize his voice. How do I recognize his voice?

"All right, can you show me?"

I wish I could see them, but I can't, only their shadows.

"Uh, no. I have to go back to my room because I need to get a few things before group movie night. You know, can't miss *50 First Dates*. Do you like Adam Sandler? I love me some Adam Sandler."

"Where is he, Tyler?"

"Right. The workout room. Gross, just extremely revolting. You better get there quickly. He might tap out on ya."

The guard doesn't say anything back, at least not anything I can hear. The heavy footsteps begin to fade as they get further down the hall. Yet Tyler's shadow remains in view. It's still and steady. I can't even see any signs of him breathing. My heart begins to race as confusion turns into paranoia.

The shadow dissipates, and he reveals himself to me bit by bit. It starts with his white sneakers and then the blue jeans that are cuffed above the laces. Then it goes to his strong right hand that's covered with hair, but even that's cut off by an orange sweater sleeve. His face comes last, and he's looking over his shoulder periodically and back to me.

I've never paid attention to Tyler before. I knew he was here, and I knew of him somewhere in this head of mine. I knew of him like I knew of Fawn because her voice is annoying and can penetrate through every wall in this building. But Tyler, his eyes are green, and the dark circles wrapped around them make him look dead inside. His hair gets cut somehow; it has to. He has a brown mop on his head that could easily turn him into Tarzan if it grows out too much. My brow rises as he lingers in front of my door.

"Hey." Tyler smiles, and I hesitantly sit up and watch his hand that's resting on my doorknob. He gives me about five seconds before shrugging and continuing to constantly look over his shoulder. "Yeah, I heard you're not much of a talker. But you and I are about to get to know each other very well. So I'm not gonna stress about it."

I squint suspiciously and hold on to my pillow for comfort for whatever he's bringing. The photos slip onto the floor as I lift it up. I hope that if I don't look down at them, he won't either. Shit, his eyes dart straight to them.

Tyler smirks and shakes his head. "Been there."

I don't say anything back. I only keep my eyes on him. He pulls out a piece of paper from his pocket and unlocks my door with a single key that he has. Then he pulls my door slightly ajar, slow enough so that it doesn't make any noise. Tyler slides the paper through the small crack he's created and shuts it back just as efficiently as he opened it.

"What is that?" I say loud enough to pass through the glass between us.

"I was never here," he replies simply, and before I know it, he's gone.

I allow a few seconds to pass, but I know if the guards see this, I'll suddenly be a patient worth paying attention to. I can't afford to be put on another drug or become more isolated than I already am. My body drops onto the floor in a cat pose, and I crawl eagerly to the paper that lies there waiting for me. Once it's in my hands, I sit crisscross applesauce with my back against the glass and unfold it.

Arlissa,

Rip this up and dispose of it when you get it.

For almost a year you've been here doing your best to cope with what you've gone through. Trust me, I

know what that feels like. Tyler went through the same thing, and he's been stuck with no promise of when he'll be let out. I know he'll buy you the time to read this, but I'll make it quick.

I will be seeing you for our session next week. But I wanted to tell you first that this will not be done the traditional way. The system isn't made to make things reasonable for people like you. But you both have a story to tell, and I'll be making sure that you get to tell it. If you trust me and you're okay with things being a little . . . unconventional . . . show up to our session. If not, I'll assign you to someone else.

T.

I fold the paper against itself twice and begin to rip it up into tiny pieces. I pick up the pictures next to it and take in a sharp inhale before pulling those apart as well. Piece by piece they go from images that trigger memories to small pieces with different colors on them.

I check the glass to make sure no one is standing there, not even Tyler, and shove the scrapped bits under my mattress. If I get out of here, I'm not going back to that life anyway.

Chapter
TWENTY-SEVEN

*D*uring downtime and in between the plethora of group activities, we all have to socialize. I don't really remember how I spent this time over the last year, but considering how people are staring at me as I walk over to the couch, I must not participate often.

Not only is it annoyingly busy here, it's also like walking through a time capsule. I wonder if it'd be better if they were all medicated psycho freaks attached to balls and chains, dragging their feet wherever they go. But no, these people wear outdated Juicy Couture and look like they robbed an Urban Outfitters. They jump up and down at the VMAs, and the girls want to be famous because they just want to be anything but who they currently are. That's the craziest part of it all. They have the same hopes, the same dreams as I did before I got here.

I wonder if they know how those same dreams can place you in the center of a crossroads. And at that center you'll be greeted by a demon who tells you they can give you everything and anything at a small price. Your soul. You ask them how long you'll be able to hold on to it—they never answer clearly.

"Someone is adjusting."

The couch sinks deeper once I realize he's here. Was he always here? Did he just sit down? Where does my mind go when I'm not there to follow?

"What?"

"She speaks!" Tyler exclaims but not loud enough to catch anyone's attention. "You cool if I sit here?" He turns and awaits my consent. Which is ridiculous considering his butt is already glued to the cushion.

"Sure, whatever. Didn't know you had manners." My vision remains on the small TV that's playing some kind of cartoon with the volume off.

"Oh, come on." He leans into the red cushion and folds his hands behind his head. "We're going to be the best of friends. Haven't you heard?"

I cross my arms over my breasts as if that will mask the way my heart is beating out of my chest. "The only thing I've heard is that you killed your entire family." That wasn't a smart thing to say.

He scoffs and raises a brow. He's looking at me, staring even. I can feel it, but I refuse to look him in the eye because then he'd have the time to take in how little I've taken care of myself. "Not entire." Tyler pauses. "I heard you killed your boyfriend."

I lift my knees into my chest and curl up on the opposite end of the couch. If I stay quiet, he might just go away.

196

"Oh, come on, that's not fair. You bring up my trauma, I bring up yours. It's banter! It could be our thing."

"I don't want to have a thing with you," I mumble into my elbow, vision persisting onto the television.

He leans in closer to me. I only know this because his breath makes the hairs on my back stand up. "Can I ask you something?"

I shake my head.

"What makes us so different? You haven't even heard my story, but at least I'm willing to hear yours." The words slide off of his tongue so well, like he rehearsed them in his room first.

I know what the note said. I know at some point I have to get to know him or my leaving this place somehow involves him. But how could I know someone who is capable of killing someone? Ending someone's life in such a cruel way?

The same way I know myself, I suppose.

I unfold myself from my position and finally turn my head to face him. He looks entertained, the smirk on his face telling me that much. "I don't have a story."

He shrugs. "Sure you do. We all have a rhyme or reason. No one is in here for fun. I mean, maybe the volunteers, but if you ask me, they're some sickos themselves."

I raise a brow and sit up a bit more, pulling on the fabric of the couch to keep me stable. "I was framed. He killed himself, so . . ."

Tyler scoffs, and his jaw practically drops to the ground. "You can pull that on anyone else, but it doesn't work with me, sweet pea. You're better off saying he was jonesing for it. But in the interest of finding common ground, I'll tell you a little something about myself."

There's a sudden thud behind us. I quickly turn to see what it is and notice one of the patients lying on the floor.

He laughs and gets right back up. "Don't you worry about me!" he exclaims and waltzes over to the chessboard as if a song is playing that only he can hear. He's a heavyset man with bald patches all around his head. The doctors watch him closely but continue to stand idly by.

"You can rely on your gut instinct, you know."

His words snap me out of my trance. "What?"

"You can rely on your gut instinct to decide whether or not someone in this room is capable of carving your eyes out with one of those spoons. You don't get that with Kimberly, who helps serve our food, or the guy who looks like he ate Pee-wee Herman over there. You damn sure don't get it with Fawn over there."

I twist my body a bit to follow where his vision goes. The small woman is chatting up some guards with the biggest smile on her face. Gross.

"But I get it with you. And you don't get it with me."

"I do."

"Eh, you don't. If you were scared of me, I'd know. Trust me, a lot of people have been scared of me." He smirks and sinks deeper into the couch. "Dr. Ryan was right; you are a terrible liar. We can work on that."

"We? Dr. Ryan?"

"Theodora. She lets us call her that because we're younger and she thinks it'll help with trust or whatever. Theodora Ryan is her full name. And she is how we'll get the fuck out of here." His tone lowers to a whisper toward the end of his sentence, and he looks around to make sure everyone is too drugged up to notice what he's saying.

"Aren't you going to tell me your life story now?"

Tyler stands and shakes his head. "Nope. Because you're not scared of me, so it'd just be, uh . . . useless information. But when you're ready to come to terms with what you did, I might just trust you enough to start this—" He pauses, and his vision lands on every corner of the room before circling back to me. He then mouths, "Prison break." Tyler chuckles and leaves me to sit on this couch, soaking up those two words.

She wasn't trying to get me out using science, a diagnosis, or finding a hole in my court documents. For all I know she has already decided on my guilt but has some reason or another to want me out of here. This isn't a decision between whether I want to embrace this life or fight for my freedom. It's a decision on whether I want to remain here or try out life as a fugitive.

I turn to the TV, where an infomercial is possibly telling me the million side effects of a specific drug. The person is sad at first, and her daughter goes to her dad and is possibly saying something along the lines of "Why isn't mommy okay?" He says something else, and suddenly I wish I knew how to read lips. The mom sobs over her unfinished artwork, and it begins to rain outside of their modern-decorated house. It's not calm rain; it's a thunderstorm. The kind of thunderstorm you don't need audio to know what it sounds like. The roaring from the clouds, the vibrations coming from thunder, and the sound of rain pounding down on your roof. Then the miserable mother takes her medication. She walks out into the rain and leaves the confines of her home. And a rainbow appears.

A week can pass by in the blink of an eye when there's something to look forward to. Although I'm not really looking forward to meeting with Dr. Ryan. I'm intrigued, curious even, but not happy about it.

There's the obvious assumption that Tyler could have been lying. But there's also a sense of resilience in him, like he's the kind of person who doesn't back down in the face of adversity. Then there's the underlying tone of unearned confidence. But then again, I don't know if it was earned. I just know that he gives me the vibe of someone whose truth you should never challenge. You could also say those are the qualities of a killer.

When we're kids, we're taught things like one plus one equals two, or that fire trucks are red and the sky is blue. We are told these things so many times by so many people that they are deemed to be true. We don't question these truths, and because the sky being blue was verified by everyone else we know and even people we don't, it's called common knowledge. Then we'll believe it when those same people we share common knowledge with tell us that their core values are our own.

Maybe I was always prone to addictions because my mom throws back a bottle of vodka like it's nobody's business. Maybe my dad's struggle with post-army PTSD is the reason why I assumed my experiences were normal for so long. Which is insane to me because there was a time when I'd rather take a razor to my skin than resemble them.

But regardless, I can have all of the self-awareness I want and still be unable to tell thought A from thought B. I can't tell if the sky is really blue or if I just made that up one day, because it feels so real to me. For all I know I'm imagining that everyone else is agreeing with me. I can't really say if Samantha actually helped me through high school, because who's to say that that's not true? Saying it's not is like saying the sky isn't blue, and it is.

A burly man escorts me through the dimmed halls that are painted an ugly coffee color. The lack of trust I have compared to most of the people here is based on performance only. If I had adjusted faster, I probably wouldn't have had to get ushered everywhere. He stops at a door that I'm familiar with now. It's a solid shade of dark chocolate, but there's a window large enough to see everything happening inside. Theodora waits there silently. Her pale hands hold on to her pen so tensely that her knuckles turn white.

The man opens the door for me, and I scuffle by him to go in. The sudden slamming sound causes me to jump a bit, but I keep my composure enough to take my seat. That door didn't look as heavy as it sounded. The same green cushion allows me to make myself comfortable in these armless seats. I keep my hands folded in front of me and wait for her to acknowledge me. Why hasn't she looked up?

"Hello?" I question, leaning forward in curiosity.

Nothing. Okay then. Not weird at all.

I let a few more seconds pass and lean back into the chair to convey disinterest. A lie, but if she's not paying attention, then neither will I. The only thing that can be heard is the pen scraping against the paper that belongs to the notebook in her lap. It's bending on both sides thanks to her using her fairly thick thighs as a table.

"Theodora?"

Her line of sight completely disregards me and goes to the door. It drops to the ground, where the gap between the door and the floor shows a large black boot. Her lips press together tightly, and she goes back to writing down whatever it is she was scribbling. Silence continues to take a seat between us, and my focus ends up falling on the clock that hangs on the wall. I watch the red hand go around over and over again. I count three full circles.

Theodora's attention goes back to the gap under the door. The boots are still there. It feels as if they're both waiting for something and I'm the only one clueless as to what that something is. She rolls her eyes and finally puts that damn pen down on the chair next to her; the notebook follows. Our eyes meet for a second, and I squint, finding myself wondering if she's real. Is any of this? Or am I in another pocket of my brain that I'm too scared to break out of?

"Good morning, Arlissa." Her sultry voice breaks through my train of thought.

"Hi."

"How are you feeling today?"

I shrug and knit my brows together in partial annoyance. "Fine."

"Have you been taking your medicine?"

"They make me sick."

"But have you been?"

"Yeah."

"Good."

"Thanks."

The six-foot-something man who was standing by the door ends up peering through the window. He doesn't look curious; in fact his face says that he's already found what he was looking for. I try to ignore him and keep my hands tucked in my lap.

"I want you to know that a clear diagnosis isn't evident yet. Your initial paperwork presents that you were in a paranoid state, emotionally distraught following the death of your boyfriend. Another doctor wants to say you have delusional disorder. The list goes on. But I don't want to focus on that. I want to focus on your current state."

It's shit. I don't need a doctor to tell me that. "Um . . . Okay?"

His head vanishes from the glass, and the sound of footsteps going down the hall fills our ears. I can tell she's paying close attention because her chin rose eagerly the moment one foot hit the ground. The steps fade out, signaling to us both that he's left. But again, what the fuck are we waiting for?

She sighs and restores her proper posture. My slumped shoulders become more presentable in response. "You've spoken to Tyler?"

I frantically turn my head around the room in an attempt to find something to let me know that this isn't a question I should answer. There's nothing. Not even a camera nailed to the ceiling. "Um, yeah."

"Then you know what we're trying to achieve here?"

"Not really?" I almost shout, but the look in her eyes tells me to quiet down. I roll my own orbs and wet my vocal cords by gulping hard for optimum whispering. "He said a few things. I read the letter, but I just don't get it. It doesn't make any sense."

Theodora nods. "I can explain."

"Please do, because he said something about . . ." I scan my surroundings again. Nothing has changed in this room, but it helps my paranoia. My body leans in as close to her as possible without falling out of my chair, and I break out a full-blown whisper. "Breaking out of here. And it's been freaking me out because there are cops and the law . . . And I am already in enough trouble with the fucking law. I've lost everything, okay? My friends, my family, my dogs. Every last thing. I'm just saying, it'd be nice to not be a fucking outlaw. I'm not Bonnie, and Tyler might want to be Clyde but he doesn't have the body count for that. And you're supposed to be a freaking doctor and prescribe me meds and tell me that I can get out of here once I'm no longer a threat and—"

"It doesn't work that way," she calmly responds.

"Huh?" I sink back into the chair due to my stomach grumbling in disapproval of my current blood pressure spike.

"I have worked in this system for a long time. I have worked with all kinds of patients. Some were almost just like you—some were like Tyler. And the fact of it is that they don't want you back out there—in the world. They make places like these comfortable and mind-numbing enough to where you no longer care to see Vegas during spring break or come and go your own accord. What you are looking at in terms of your future is what Tyler already has. And do you see a life you're envious of? He gets to go out sometimes. Maybe he'll even get a day job at the fast-food chain down the street one day. They will do absolutely anything to make the thought of sleeping anywhere but here one that feels impossible."

I find myself on the verge of tears, like a river being held back by a dam made of paper. "Why are you telling me this?"

"Because I want you to come with us."

"Us?"

"Tyler can't leave without me, and I won't be leaving him in here. I'd like for you to come, seeing as we have similar goals."

I shake my head in disbelief and lazily wipe a tear that's escaped from my right eye. "What goals?"

"Just say yes. A yes that you'll do what it takes. You've been chosen, Arlissa. You believe in God, right?"

"Yes."

"And he hasn't left you. Instead he's spared you for something important."

"But I'll spend the rest of my life running."

"Isn't that better than being alone? I've checked your reports, files, and logs. You received your first visitor only a few weeks ago. A visitor that logged in under an alias, and

I know they weren't a parent. You're already alone. With us you'll have support—people to depend on."

"Why do you want Tyler out? He killed his entire family . . . That's more people—"

"Than you killed?"

My mouth hangs open while I try to process the fact that she said that. I don't want to say it's true. I can't even think that's true. "Huh?"

"We are beyond not being honest with each other, Arlissa. I need that if Tyler and I can trust you."

"Trust me? You're joking, right?"

She nonchalantly shakes her head. "You're projecting. Let's circle back."

My lip begins to quiver. I bite down hard on the bottom one to avoid her noticing. "What do you want from me?"

"I want you to want this."

"Of course I don't want to fucking be here. Who does?"

"Then I need you to admit it. Claim it. Accept that God has given you a chance to achieve deliverance. Become one with what you've done because you will have to be that same person to help me get you out of here."

"Why?"

"Because that person was capable of anything. Don't you want to be her again? Free? Out of the United States and somewhere people aren't sneaking a picture of you for the tabloids every five seconds? Or calling you crazy? Or not trusting you with real silverware? You can start over, Arlissa. Be whoever you want to be. And I know how to make that happen for you."

"What if they come looking?"

"They won't."

I bite down on my nail again in hesitation. "How do you know?"

"Trust me. I just need you to admit it. I've been watching you for months. That state of delusion you spent the entirety of your time here in was quite telling. This confession is haunting you, and harboring that truth is keeping you from breaking free of it completely. You feel like you have to be on trial, don't you? But what if I told you that you don't have to face anyone?"

I roughly wipe off any tears that have escaped, and my cheeks sting because of it. This all feels bogus, even crazier than my dream world. Is this some kind of new strategy to get me to admit the one thing I've already been sent away for? Or is truth really stranger than fiction?

It's a chance.

I jump in my seat as the whisper comes in full blast in my head. My eyes shut briefly, and my head drops into my hands.

"Are you okay?" I can hear Theodora say, but she's not what I want to listen to right now. It's Samantha. The only person who can guide me in the right direction. "What's going on? Talk to me."

It's a chance to start over. It's not traditional, but it's a chance. If it fails, then what? You end up right back here anyway. You have nothing to lose.

"But what about . . . What about him?" I mutter into my hands.

"Arlissa? Come on, come back to me."

You have to be honest about what you know, what you remember.

I look up with pure dismay written on my face. My mouth opens, and only air comes out at first. I have to. I have to take this chance. I have to do what Samantha says. "We argued that night . . . After, um, sleeping together. I was falling asleep, and since we had just gotten out of a huge argument, I wanted him to . . . stay with me. I, uh, I wanted him to stay. But he got up. I don't know why. I mean I know why. He wanted to get high. And usually I didn't protest against those things, but he had . . . He was starting to or always had and maybe I just didn't notice a heroin kick. Thing. He had a problem with heroin."

"Okay . . . Go on."

I sheepishly go limp and pull some loose hairs behind my ear. "That's what he wanted to do. And I never said anything before, but this time I was so . . . I was upset. So I yelled at him, and he told me he would rather kill himself than be with me . . . And I don't . . . I don't remember. I just remember waking up, and I found him. But it took me this long to remember that much. A year ago, I forgot the argument even happened."

"Is that the real story?"

"It's the only one I know."

I received a rundown on how I could assist with this project—without the details of the project. It's not a breakout, it's a project. Theodora thinks I will wrap my head around it easier if I see it that way. Genuinely, I don't think they trust me with the nuts and bolts of this operation yet. However, being a part of something for the few hours as I have been has distracted me from the grief that weighs heavily on my heart. I carry it like it hurts, and anyone with two eyes can see that.

Instead of thinking about Xavier, I focus on the to-do list that was verbally given to me by Dr. Ryan.

Task 1: Become a Model Patient (Slowly. Not so fast that it's suspicious.)

Task 1, sub B (assigned to me, by me): Figure Out Tyler.

Being held up in a place where everyone is accounted for isn't the worst thing when you're looking for someone. State supervision doesn't have many perks, but it has that one.

I'm escorted to what reminds me of a high school cafeteria. I go through the line to receive my daily serving of cold eggs and a single piece of toast to eat with a spoon. My brown orbs try not to make it too obvious that I'm searching for him. I take a seat in the furthest right corner, where I haven't seen anyone sit since my arrival. Not that I've been paying attention—I could be stealing someone's seat for all I know. I slide my body in between the hard wood that gets dubbed a seat and the slightly higher piece that's called a table. The eggs jiggle when the plate hits the surface. I pick up my spoon and pretend to eat while the nurses and guards survey the area for any misbehavior. Why isn't he here yet? No one is allowed to sleep in.

I store my end goal in the back of my mind and begin eating my ice-cold food. My fragile teeth bite down on the toast, and the crunch shocks me a bit. Crumbs gather on my gray top in tiny pieces. Today, I went for a long-sleeve shirt and sweatpants instead of my prison-feeling sweatsuit. I quickly brush the crumbs off of the fabric and onto the ground. Before I can register how much time has passed, my plate is empty and a nurse is hovering over me.

"Time for your medicine, Arlissa. I see you've changed your seat."

I wipe my face and nod. "Yeah."

Her blotched blue dye job from a few weeks ago is gone. Real Evelyn's dry strands are now subjected to the torture of being a mousy brown. She places the pills next to my plate and gives me a kid-size cup of water. "Go on," she commands, stepping back to allow me my space but not far enough to not see me swallow.

A model patient takes her medicine. Even when she doesn't know what it's for. The palm of my hand greets the two tablets before I throw my head back and toss them down my throat. I grab the water and gulp it down as fast as possible. My eyes remain on the patients eating their breakfast. Those who have made friends engage in what looks like interesting conversation. They've all forgotten what life really is about.

"Good job." Real Evelyn is pleased enough to pick up my plate and cup for me. "Will you be going to group today? Seems you're ready for it."

"Um . . ." I want to ask which one, but I don't really feel like looking like an idiot. I roughly rub my hands along my thighs sheepishly instead.

"You're nervous. I get it. You've been out of it for a while, and I understand how overwhelming this can be. Goals group is very quick, only fifteen minutes after breakfast every morning. You can meet the other pat—" She pauses and bites the inside of her cheek, "You can meet your peers and set goals for the day. You don't have to talk if you don't want to, but I know Dr. Ryan would appreciate knowing you're participating before you see her again." Her eyes twinkle as if there's more under the surface than what's actually coming out of her mouth.

"Okay." I remove myself from the bench by taking one foot out and then the other. The nurse looks pleased as she guides me through the cafeteria. I take one last subtle look around before we exit the large space completely—no Tyler. I roll my eyes in the split second that I have to myself without Real Evelyn studying my body language. My right hand holds onto my left tricep as we hurry through the halls.

"Here we are." She pushes open another dark chocolate door that announces my presence to a room with a few chairs and a whiteboard. A man sits at a desk by the board and raises his head once he notices us.

"Oh, hello." He gets up and quickly pats off his sweater vest. "I'm Dr. Fell. Will you be joining us today?" He looks me dead in the eyes, heavy facial hair only providing a distraction.

"Arlissa is getting used to the group environment, and we thought attending Goals this morning would be a good start."

"Well, that's amazing. Go ahead and take a seat while we wait for the rest of the group. They should be done with breakfast in about . . . three minutes, right?"

Real Evelyn nods in agreement. "You got it."

Dr. Fell smiles. "All right, thank you. I'll take it from here. You can sit wherever you want. No one really claims any of the chairs. Well, no one but Tyler Evans."

I take small steps around the room that smells less like a clinic than the others have. This one carries a hint of mint in the air, but it could also be from the cologne he's wearing. I take my seat as far in the back of the room as I can get. Dr. Fell returns to his desk, where he places his glasses back on the bridge of his nose and returns to his paperwork. He must not care for small talk. I can appreciate that.

One by one, different people come in. He greets them all by name, and that's how I learn not only theirs but his first name as well. Melinda comes in first. She's got long legs and wears neon leggings to show them off. She's the one who calls Dr. Fell by his first name—Patrick. After her comes Washington, an overweight man with rich umber skin who reminds me of my dad if he never went through basic training. I'm sure Washington isn't his first name, but no one is brave enough to confirm my theory. Amber comes in smiling, high-fiving everyone who looks open to it. Greggory, Hector, Miles, and Kent come in as a group of their own. Fawn comes in skipping shortly after—I already know her name and how annoying she is. But I didn't know about her attraction to fire, and that's how she got here.

I stop taking note of everyone's name and fun facts and settle into my corner while almost all of them (except Washington) join in conversation with each other. I give up on patrolling the door when Dr. Fell gets up to shut it fully.

His hand pushes on the heavy wood but stops when a single black sneaker acts as a door stopper. "You're late, Tyler."

Tyler rolls his eyes playfully, and a smug smile graces his features. "Fashionably. Had a bit of a rough morning, Doc." He comes into full view and allows the door to shut behind him. His long pointer finger draws attention to the credit-card-sized bandage on his neck.

"Glad you're okay. Please take your seat."

"Aw, man, really, Fawn? My seat? I guess since I'm the latest chicken to the race, I'll sit in the back with—" His eyebrows rise, and his light orbs twinkle when he catches sight of me. "The newbie."

No one really pays him any attention when he slides past their chairs to the only empty one next to me. He leans over and almost catches me staring at the bandage on his neck. What the hell happened?

"Hey," he whispers, but his gaze remains on the front of the room, where Dr. Fell is beginning to speak.

"All right, guys. As always, we only have fifteen minutes before you're off for the rest of the day. Let's get around the room quickly. Make sure you have at least one goal in mind when I get to you—no matter how small. No pressure. And like always, you have until I see you next to complete it."

"Hi," I respond to Tyler as Dr. Fell begins to point them out one by one.

"Um, to keep down lunch today."

"I don't know, to take a walk."

"Finish my book!"

"Win a game of chess."

"Uh . . . Pass?"

He continues to go around the room until he gets to Fawn, who is right before Tyler. "I'm going to have a great day!"

Tyler smirks. "My turn already? Wow. I think I'll show my new friend Arlissa here the ropes."

My mouth goes wide open to make the shape of an O. I quickly close it and wiggle uncomfortably in my chair.

"That's great, Tyler. Arlissa?"

"Um. I guess . . . Try to do better."

"That's a good one, thank you."

He returns to the whiteboard and begins jotting down his favorite ones in blue. Tyler's goes at the top of the list as: "Help others adapt."

Chapter
THIRTY

*T*he clouds hovering over us feel lower than I ever remember them being. Whenever I glance out of the small window in my room, I can see that there are acres of forest beyond these walls. The wind blows toward me, and my stray hairs dance to its rhythm. The sun streams through the trees and greets me with a warmth that I haven't experienced in a long time. Longer than before Xavier died.

I don't know when I decided to sit on the grass, but it happened and it feels good. If I were barefoot, I'd curl my toes in between the blades and pick up as much soil as possible. I'm no longer concerned about bugs or dirt like I used to be. I'm more focused on how much I missed the feeling of cool soil under my butt no matter how warm it is outside.

"You good?"

I don't know how long Tyler has been crouched over me, but he is. My orbs take in his denim wash jeans and the bright green shirt that's one size too big.

"You seem far away."

"I can't remember the last time I felt the sun," I whisper. Wow, that sounded weird as hell. I shake it off and rise to my feet.

He follows my action, hovering over me with almost a foot more than my height. It's not that hard to tower over me, though. Especially considering there are children taller than me. "You don't have to act like you didn't say that, you know."

"Say what?"

Tyler laughs and beckons me to begin walking the perimeter of the garden. "You're funny."

Security and orderlies watch our behavior; I make the conscious effort to drop my shoulders and unclench my jaw. "Can we get to the point?"

Tyler skips backward, and I'm forced to jog next to him. "What point?"

"What are we doing right now? Why are you acting like everything is so . . . normal?"

The male slows down his pace and turns back around so that we're facing the same direction. "I want to introduce you to someone. They're right over there." He points to a guard who is already walking toward us.

"Who is that?"

Tyler leans in but keeps his vision locked on the skinny man making fast steps to us. "You want an in? Fine. Show me I can trust you and don't stop talking."

The guard whose name tag reads "Samuel" collides with Tyler. We end up under a large oak tree that feels cut off from the rest of the group. They both quickly recover, and that cocky smile Tyler holds comes right back. "Sam! Samuel. Buddy ol' pal. I want to introduce you to someone."

"Arlissa Benson. I'm aware. Hello."

"H-hi."

I watch as Tyler eases to the guy's right side. "You've never been out here before, have you?"

"No. It's been . . . strange? Really hard. I don't know what I thought would happen if I didn't snap out of—my delusions. But here I am, so . . ." Don't stop talking. "I don't regret it, though. This place isn't that bad . . . I've, um, accepted that. I'm just trying to be happy here. Happier than before."

Samuel easily feeds into every word I say, as if he would rather be one of the doctors than just a guard making sure we don't carve each other's eyes out with a spoon. "I see. Well, let's hope the sun helps."

"Exactly. But sometimes I'm scared that nothing I say will really matter because—" I watch as Tyler's hand falls to the key ring looped around the man's belt loop. I look around to see no one around us at all. Sam leans back on his heels, and Tyler quickly locks both hands behind his back. "Because . . ." His eyes connect with mine, and he widens them as if I'm meant to get some sort of signal. "I'm sorry, my medicine just—" I press my hand against my head, and Samuel's bushy brows come together in confusion. Without thinking, I propel my body forward, and both men attempt to grab me.

"Whoa there, are you all right? I'm going to call the doctor," Sam says as he helps me get back on my feet.

"Yeah, yeah. I just get dizzy sometimes. I think it's a side effect. You don't have to call anyone."

"No, I'll get you to the doctor before lunch."

"I'm sure I'm—"

"Oh wow, we almost lost ya there!" Tyler exclaims before quickly stuffing what is probably one of those bronze keys in his pocket.

Samuel glares at Tyler, and Tyler just rolls his eyes as if there's something the two have against each other. "Time's about up anyway. You guys get inside."

"Aye, aye, captain. Come on, Arlissa."

He doesn't touch me like I'm used to. If Xavier wanted something, he'd command it and wrap an arm around me to ensure I really got the message. Tyler just trusts that I'll follow—and I do.

"What was that?" I whisper while we both slide through the door that's being held open by one of the guards.

"We have one week," he responds as we hurry through the halls. The others who were out with us go the normal way to the cafeteria, but Tyler instead makes a sharp right.

"For what?"

"By next Sunday morning, you won't be waking up here. Neither of us will."

"Is that what you needed the key for?" My eyes take in the wing that I've never been to before. It looks darker, scarier, and the doors are steel and larger than the ones that I remember.

"No. They change those once they realize one is gone. We'll probably have about a day. Plus, that won't get us out the doors. The key is more useful for another reason than opening an actual d—" Tyler's voice trails off as he comes face-to-face with another guard.

My heart races once I notice that the man is on the other side of the hall with the clear intention of stopping us.

Tyler keeps speeding toward him, and at this point all I can do is follow. He comes to a quick halt and nods at the balding guy with a beer belly. "I got it."

His face is stuck on me but only looks away for a moment to speak to Tyler. "Why is she here?"

"She's coming."

The stranger bites his cheek, and in this stalemate he gives me enough time to notice his name tag. Logan. "I thought it was just you."

"And I thought you had more sense than to just stand here and talk," he challenges.

The older man backs down and returns to his initial train of thought. "You got the key?"

"That's what I said."

"Okay. That'll be enough to get Samuel fired."

"Good, I hope the bastard doesn't think I forgot. I still have a scar on my back."

"He's a good man."

Tyler scoffs. "You're kidding, right? I was fourteen when he beat me with an iron bar because I was just another fucked up kid."

"You were also around that age when you murdered a bunch of people. We all do shit, Tyler."

"Good one, and good riddance. Don't send a Christmas card. Well, not that I'll hand him over a forwarding address. Now, what time?"

"I'm thinking around midnight. Samuel usually has the graveyard shift on the weekends, and since you've gotten 'bout a quarter of the staff fired already and twice as many have quit . . ." His vision shifts to the bandage on Tyler's neck, but he quickly goes back to making eye contact. "Staffing that shift is going to be a bitch. There won't be many people left to cover all the exits. I took the shifts for all next week, so I'll be able to briefly cut the cameras off. What about Fawn?"

Tyler pushes his lips out and waves his hand down. "Don't worry about her. I got that all taken care of."

What the hell does annoying-ass Fawn have to do with anything?

"Good. And Theodora?"

"She's ready."

"Cool. And how are we getting *her* out?" His head nudges in my direction, and my heart skips a beat.

Tyler's eyes scan me from head to toe before a creepy smile appears on his face. He has a pretty smile. I never noticed that before.

"Easy. But you don't worry about that part. Just play yours, and we'll play ours."

"All right. You guys head on back, I suggest from different directions. I'll follow to give anyone a reasonable explanation."

Tyler clicks his tongue and pats the other guy on the shoulder before heading back up the hall. I follow him until we get to a T-section where we can go left or right. Logan keeps a lazy pace behind us.

"I'll go to the right since I know this place better than you. You head back to the cafeteria. If anyone asks, you had to go to the restroom. You were feeling dizzy. Samuel can back that up. Go see a doctor if you have to. I'll go this way since I know what to avoid."

"Hey," I call out before he runs off.

"Yeah?"

"What happened to you? With the other guard?"

The smile returns. "Pull this off for us and I'll tell you the entire heart-wrenching CNN crime-time story."

I nod, not because I agree but because challenging him doesn't make much sense. None of this does. Yet in a strange way I feel more in control of my free will than I did in my dreams. I can do this. Not because I can but because I want to. And that much power is dangerous.

The only time I'm happy is four seconds after I wake up. Before I've remembered who I am or what my life is about. But now I have a reason to get out of bed in the morning. A reason beyond the judging eyes of the nurses who are telling me I need to bathe.

When you actually have a lust to see the next day, you move differently, you breathe differently. You start to care about the strands in your hair being out of place because life is more than just eating a meal to stay alive. You start to think about the future, which is a dangerous game, but a game to be played nonetheless.

I woke up this morning and pulled at my lips to expose my inflamed gums. I pinched my cheeks that aren't as chubby as they used to be from the weight I've lost. Not that I had much body weight to begin with, but now I'm skin and bones. I spent more time staring at my reflection and trying to figure out what I'll do with my new freedom than I did when I was actually free. I imagined all the possibilities; whether I'm hiding out in Oklahoma or wearing large hats in Mexico, it'll all feel the same. I'll be better. And that promise is strong enough to paint the colors of my rainbow.

"Ms. Benson, you have a visitor," the guard says. I didn't even hear him unlock and open my door.

"It's early," I respond. I hope it's not Alejandra, especially not after the unfortunate interaction we had just weeks ago. Plus, I don't know if I can look anyone else in the eye who somehow participated in my large-scale delusion. A delusion. That's all it was. A sequel to a life I no longer have. A place where everyone played a more interesting part than the one they actually do—me included.

"Let's go." The guard exhales as if I'm a walking inconvenience. I recognize him from somewhere—but I can't put my finger on it.

"Okay," I whisper and quickly slip on my laceless shoes. He lets the door slam behind me and grabs my arm with a grip that sends me back to Xavier's same iron-tight hold. He drags me down the hall even though I am more than capable of walking on my own. There's an aggression with every step he takes—a tiredness, as if I made him do this.

I can't tell whether I feel angry or scared or nothing at all. He squeezes my arm tighter once we turn a corner, and I wince ever so quietly. I want him to let go, but he doesn't. I've been to this room once before, but this time the journey is more daunting than the first.

When we arrive, he tosses my arm in order to use his key card to unlock the immense glass door. I can't see who is waiting for me on the other side yet; only the yellow paint that coats the walls is in my view.

"You have fifteen minutes," he plainly commands, his voice sounding like thunder, and I'm too rattled to even give a response.

All I can do is cup my hands together in front of my waist and walk through the sliding doors. They slam shut behind me. There's another guard in the corner keeping watch, but the one that escorted me remains outside. I look over the empty tables and chairs, one after the other. No one yet. I turn to face the furthest corner of the room, and what I see almost knocks me down to my knees.

She's gained some weight since I last saw her. Okay, a lot of weight. But the pixie cut she cut her hair into over a year ago still remains the same. She's settling into old age well. The haircut really does the trick. Oh, hey, she's wearing the red blouse I got her for Christmas a few years ago. I remember it like it was yesterday. I got it from the one time Xavier and I participated in Paris Fashion Week. I never got to experience many of those, and now neither of us will experience them anymore.

"Mom?"

A sympathetic smile forms on her lips, and she quickly corrects her posture. I can see her debating whether she wants to stand or not. Honestly, I don't know how I'm even standing, considering I can no longer feel my legs. This is the first time I'm seeing her since—I don't know. I can't remember.

"Hi, honey. You look well." She's lying. I can tell because there are tears flooding her eyes. She sniffles in an attempt to keep them at bay, but I'm not an idiot.

"Thanks." It's all I can say as I take a seat across from her. What would be a moment of joy is instead a moment of confusion and bubbling rage. At what point do we speak about the fact that I have been in here alone? At what point do we acknowledge that I lost a year to this place because I had nothing to hold on to in my doomed reality? At what point do we get to blame our mothers?

"How are you holding up?"

"You'd know if you were here," I spit out, unsure where the aggression is coming from. Maybe years of walking through middle school and high school with a bloody keychain because my mother never hugged me through my grief. Maybe from the year of being in here because she was out there probably drinking herself to death and disassociating from the sick irony of one kid being killed and the other being a killer. I have a right to be angry, and she doesn't have an excuse.

"I wanted to be . . . I promise. But you have to understand it was hard to process, and I did try! I did try to come one day. But they told me you weren't in a good space. You had been fighting and needed to be sedated. And, baby, that terrified me, okay? I felt like I didn't know who you were, and I failed. I failed, and I am here to make peace with that." She begins to choke up, and her soft southern accent birthed from North Carolina only comes across as pitiful now. "You know, your daddy and I started going to church again. And he would have loved to be here, but he's gotten tied up with somethings but—but he'll be here."

I sit there with a blank stare on my face. How can she expect me to sympathize with that? "You both didn't speak to me for a year. You tried to see me once. And they told you those things and you ran. How long ago was that?"

Shame washes over her face, and her cheeks begin to flush. "In August."

"A fucking month?" I exclaim. The guard pushes closer to us. I lean back to make as much space between her and me as I can.

"Now you watch your language."

"Fuck no. I've been in here, and you don't think I've needed someone? I needed my mom. I couldn't stay awake. I couldn't tell . . . day from night. I couldn't—" I sharply exhale and try to find peace with my emotions, but they're all chaotic. "I couldn't live like this. I was so scared to come to terms with the fact that this was my life and I had no one. You, Dad, Aly. My manager dumped me. I found out Ellie died because those sick nurses were trying to get me to say literally anything. That's how I found out. And I had no one for that. I didn't deserve that. I didn't deserve to get thrown away like both of your children died."

"You don't bring Samantha into this. What happened to her has nothing to do with what you did to that boy."

My head moves in a slow nod as I process what just came out of her mouth. "What do you want?"

"I want to take you home, baby. I know you're angry and scared, and I understand."

"You don't. You're not in here."

"I know, but . . . I have some news. Some good news that'll help us put this all behind us." She wipes her tears and leans forward across the table. "There was some talk from your lawyer to me about some missing discovery. It looks like the case was tampered with that prevented you from getting a fair trial. And maybe—there may be a chance of—you coming home, Lissa. You coming back to Nevada, and we forget this ever happened."

"No one will forget."

"You won't know until you try."

"And what? I go through this trial that might happen and maybe hope for the best? A year later everyone is reminded of what happened? I get thrown back in here? Or they say I'm fucking fine and I go to jail instead? I won't get to model again. I can't go back to Carson City. I can't stay in California. Where do I go? Where do I go to be normal?"

"You go home. Maybe we can stay with my mom in North Carolina. She'd be thrilled to have you."

My bottom lip quivers at the thought. "I don't want that."

"What better choices do you have, Arlissa? Look around. Look at where you are."

Dr. Ryan's words interrupt my thoughts. Acknowledge what I did. Be that person because that person will get me out of this. She wasn't wrong. Ridiculous-sounding, probably, but not wrong. I'm better when I own up to the reason—the truth. My story.

My tone lowers so that the only person who can hear me is my mom. "See, that's the thing, Mom. I have been. I've taken the last few days, and I've really seen where I am. I was fighting for myself when he died. Because he beat me down in ways that I still don't understand. Sometimes I'm eating breakfast and I remember the little things he'd do to make me someone he wanted me to be. And here I might be medicated and locked down, but I know who I am. And if I go through that trial? If we somehow get that far? His entire family can just change the damn narrative again. I'd rather rot in here. Where no one can change the story."

She remains frozen with her elbows glued to the table. Disbelief is drawn across her face as if an artist came in and perfectly posed her. It goes away quickly, though. My mother clears her throat and takes in a deep inhale and releases an audible exhale. "In one week, your lawyer would like a response as to if you'd like to move forward. I'll be back Monday morning, and I hope you make the right choice. I just . . . I hope you choose to be with your family. Don't let this year beat you down. And I am so sorry that I wasn't there. I should have been, and I'm not only talking about the last year. Just remember that you will always have choices. And you are my little girl. My baby. You will always make the right one."

I furrow my brows and get up from the seat. I don't care to look back to see her as I swiftly make my way to the glass door and bang on it twice. The guard on the other side unlocks the door, and I start walking down the hall before he can touch me. He doesn't try again. He instead walks behind me, his heavy boots the only sound I can hear.

We all have choices. I just have to be sure of mine.

Chapter
THIRTY-TWO

I stand idly by while patients in Abercrombie and Fitch do their daily laps. I switched out my normal gray sweatshirt for an orange one. I have a few random clothing items that I can't quite tell where they came from. I don't feel right wearing them. At least I didn't; not until now. When going through the few things I do have, I also noticed a burgundy sweatshirt. It wasn't mine. I understand the confusion, though. It was Xavier's. I had left it at my mother's house after visiting for her birthday, and now it's somehow made its way back to me. I stopped believing in signs a long time ago. But that might be one.

"Good morning!" Fawn sings as she skips by me and begins walking the grassy perimeter. I can't tell if she's talking to me or literally everyone around me. I nod to be polite, but I can't stand her. Why? I don't know. But everyone else nods and smiles, some guards even watching her as if she's America's Next Top Model. They'd notice if she was gone. Me? Not so much.

"Get moving, Benson," the guard with the attitude barks.

"I'm not feeling too well," I lie. Reality being that I need to catch Tyler and use the time we have to get some answers out of him.

"You look just fine. Go on or head back inside." He waves me away. I want to pout but opt for doing what I'm told instead.

"Oh, come on, Robert. You gotta learn to be nicer these days."

The voice chimes in behind me, and my snail-paced walking comes to a quick halt. I place a hand over my forehead to shield my eyes from the sun, and there he is. He has a new bandage on today. His last one was stained brown with old blood by the time dinner came around.

"Tyler, help me get them in line. Samuel is out, and I'm the only one out here today," he pleads. Robert speaks to him with a kind of respect that I never get. Instead, I get dragged through the halls like I'm the worst thing that ever happened to him.

"Samuel's out? He sick or something?" Tyler questions. His line of sight falls on me briefly before returning to his conversation.

"Something like that." Robert shakes his head in disapproval and then shoots his glare in my direction. "Benson! Walk!"

Tyler clicks his tongue a few times and pats the man on the back. "Don't worry. I got 'er."

The lanky man nods and walks away to bother someone else instead of verifying that Tyler will stick to his word. But he does. Once he's at my side, he runs his hands through his hair and ushers me to follow him. "Waiting for me?"

"Actually, yes. Do you know that guard?"

"I've been here a decade. I know everyone."

"Yeah, but like . . . know him. Like Logan." I stress the word *know* in hopes that he understands what I'm trying to say.

"Oh, no." He chuckles. "But he did save my ass when Samuel was beating me to a pulp. He's got a wife he hates, but he ain't all that bad."

I frown. "Oh. Well, I have to ask you something."

"Shoot."

We make it halfway around the property to the old tree where Samuel's key was stolen. There is only a gate separating us from the normal world across the street. There's a basketball court. I wonder if children play there sometimes. Children like Hope.

"Hello. Earth to Arlissa."

"Right." I stand up straight and continue walking to maintain the space between us and the other patients. "I need to know."

"How many licks it takes to get to the center of a Tootsie Pop?" He scratches his cheek nonchalantly as his long legs pull him forward.

"No. What you did. Why you did it. I need to know before we . . . you know."

He comes to a halt, but his face doesn't say shock at all. "I told you. After."

"Well, I'm telling you now, Tyler."

The male looks around to see where the minds of the twenty-something people out here are. No one is paying attention, so we remain in this spot for a bit more. "Remind me why this matters?"

"It matters to me."

"Ah, but what matters to you doesn't matter to me."

"It should. I know your plan. I know what you're doing."

He stuffs his hands in his jean pockets and rocks back and forth on his heels. "And what makes you think *that* matters?"

I bite the inside of my bottom lip and stand tall in my stance. "It matters because whatever it is is why you want me to come. Why not Fawn? You know her."

"I do. She's sort of my girlfriend." He shrugs the same way Xavier used to when Savannah was brought up. But then he showcases a goofy smile as if it's a joke.

"Oh." I look to my left and fully take in the ditzy woman with dirty-blond hair talking to anyone who will listen. She has two full tattoo sleeves that get cut off by her shirt, but she does her best to show them off.

"Your point?"

"I want to trust you. I want to know."

"Wow, you want my life story during recess? I for one value my physical activity, so I'm not too sure if I'm willing to participate."

"And I value knowing something that proves that you aren't going to leave me behind."

He tips his head back, and a wide smile replaces his straight face. "Would you look at that! I must be rubbing off already! Fine. You can have your story time, Benson. It's not that great of one anyway." He picks back up his speed, and I have to double my steps to keep up.

"So talk."

"It was a cold winter in California." He chuckles unpleasantly and wets his lips.

"I'm serious!" I shout as we make a full circle and pass Robert and a nurse who are too stuck on each other to pay much attention.

"You ever heard of Evans?"

"Like the lotions and soaps for babies and stuff?"

"Bingo!"

"What does that have to do with you?"

"You are looking at the rightful owner of that fortune."

"You're a trust fund baby . . ."

"Now who said you weren't all the way there? Not this guy. Anyway, I *was* a trust fund baby. The money went to my sister after my parents—you know. *Cleek.*"

"But you killed your whole family."

"All but one. My older sister. And turns out they didn't include all the terms and conditions in their will of if they were randomly murdered by their child and their oldest decided to forgive him. I call that a loophole."

"How did you—"

"Kill six people in the middle of the day at thirteen years old? Easily. But you don't care about the how as much as you care about the why." Tyler starts walking backward again, this time in front of me. "You want to know if they deserved it." I remain quiet. "Doesn't matter if they did or not, you know. It won't make you feel any better."

"Did you regret it?"

Tyler scoffs and runs his hands through his thick hair. "Fuck no. Are you joking?"

"Okay . . . Then what was so bad that they deserved that?"

"I was trying to get there, but you keep interrupting.

Anyway, we were filthy rich. Old money rich off of fucking soap and lotions that I used to jack my dick off. You know? Whatever. Things were cool, but my dad was a fucking terror. My mom was too passive to do anything about it. He gave her everything she had, so if I pissed him off, then I was the problem."

"Sounds like—"

"Xavier Amari. Ding ding, you got it. We went to the same school, actually."

"You knew Xavier?"

"Yup. Not as much as you, obviously. But I knew enough. Played on the same Little League team. Kid was terrible at sports. I don't know how he faked it. Fucking nepotism."

I stop in my tracks and try to force down the gulp of vomit that wants to come up from the pit of my stomach. "Oh."

"Come on, don't fake out on me yet. It's just now getting good."

I return to my normal pace while he's practically bouncing on two legs. "'Kay."

"Our parents were friends for obvious reasons. But when I got too hard to handle and the normal PG-13 abuse wasn't working, they called Bruno for some lovely parenting advice. I was like ten at this point. The only bad seed out of all my siblings. I mean, the only one who even cared to see if I was okay was Teddy."

"Teddy?"

"My older sister. She was always there—until she got sent off to boarding school. And then I was alone." His vision trails off to the blades of grass but returns to me swiftly. "Anyway. It was Bruno's idea to start tranqing me."

"Your parents *tranquilized* you?"

"Yup. For two long fucking years. So I killed them."

There's more. There has to be. But from the way he distances himself from me, I won't find out today. "So why me?"

"Because you hurt them. And that makes you someone worth knowing."

"And your older sister?"

"She wasn't in the media because they didn't want me to possibly get out of here and . . ." He cuffs his hands together and motions to his stomach as if he was stabbing himself. "Ya know? But little did they know, she wanted to find me."

"Why your other siblings? Because they were better behaved than you?"

"When you grow up in a household where your parents make you eat dog food even though they have steak and caviar for breakfast, and beat you with broomsticks—you want your siblings to be on your side. And they were, for a while. At least I thought so. Until they were holding me down . . . time after time . . . after time . . . after time."

"Didn't you love them?"

"Love is fickle, Arlissa. You of all people should know that."

"I never had any other siblings . . . Well, nothing other than my big sister, and sometimes I wish I did."

Tyler squints as he attempts to read my emotionless features. "Did that make you feel any better?"

"No," I whisper, unable to look him in the eye now.

"I told you. Listen, kid. I'm sure he deserved whatever was coming to him. And if you're wondering if he didn't because he probably grew up like me—it doesn't matter. At the end of the day, no one cares about your reasoning. It's all bullshit. You could kill me right now somehow, some-way, and no one would think twice about me by the time the sun sets tomorrow. It's just the fact that you're capable. That's what people can't look past."

I swallow hard and try to rinse out the bad taste in my mouth. "How'd you do it?"

Tyler raises a brow but chooses to answer anyway. "Knife."

"My mom visited me." My mouth releases the words before my brain can censor them. Something about him makes me want to talk, and I can't put my finger on what it is. "She said there's a possibility I could get out of here."

"Did she say there might be another trial?"

"Yeah."

"Eh. I don't want to see you go down with this place, so pick what you want. We only have a few days."

"What . . . What do you mean go down with this place?" Offense coats my words, but I lower my tone once I see I've caught the attention of a nurse.

He leans in, and the scent of vanilla coats the neckline of his T-shirt. "Can I tell you a secret?"

"What?"

"Theodora has my trust fund."

My eyes widen as the dots begin to connect. Teddy is Dr. Ryan. Dr. Ryan is his sister.

"Round up! We're going inside!" the guard shouts before I can get another word out, and Tyler gets escorted away due to Fawn tugging on his arm. I'm left again with flooding thoughts that I can't express to anyone else. My new medicine has taken off my sister-talking training wheels, and for once, I truly know how it feels to be alone.

Chapter
THIRTY-THREE

A private session with Dr. Ryan comes shortly after my chilling conversation with Tyler. I sit in my normal green chair and unfortunately arrive before her. This hasn't happened before. My eyes find the clock hung on the wall: 2:59. I'll have a minute to myself at the very least. A minute to nibble on the chilling confessions that fell out of Tyler's mouth so callously. He wasn't sad—not until he brought up what they did to him. I think, from the smiles on his face, that he was proud.

That's what makes him and me different. He's not ashamed, but I am.

The door practically flies open as Dr. Ryan comes stumbling in with all of her paperwork pressed against her chest. Her glasses are falling off, and her hair is frazzled as she walks past me and takes a seat. "Whew! It has been a day."

The longer she takes to shuffle her belongings and get settled, the less patient I am. Her hair falls out of the bun she lazily placed it in as she tries her best to mask the sound of heavy breathing.

"Why didn't you tell me you're Tyler's sister?"

A loud thud echoes throughout the room because her phone has slipped out of her hands. She places one hand on the cushion before sitting, and I notice that her nail polish matches the shade of green that coats these uncomfortable seats. The rest of her body follows, and she plops down. Theodora swipes the strands that stuck to her lip gloss out of the way and rests her eyes on me. "You two are getting quite close, then."

"No. I don't think so," I respond while returning her intrigued look with a relatively bleak one.

"Hm. I assume you want some sort of answer from me."

"No. I mean, yeah actually. Like why are your last names different?" My voice shakes. Something about her is more unsettling than Tyler himself.

She flashes a ring on her left hand. "He died from colon cancer."

"Oh. Sorry."

"He's a good guy, you know," Dr. Ryan nonchalantly says as she lifts her branded coffee cup to her lips.

"Who?"

"My brother. Our parents were never good. They often forgot about us but would keep having kids, and I didn't know why. I couldn't imagine a good reason why. And being the oldest in that situation . . . You just want to fix it, take them away somehow. I'm sure your sister felt that way about you."

"What?"

Theodora exhales casually and pulls open one of the folders that are scattered in the pile of papers she brought with her. "You spoke a lot when you weren't too present. I learned more about you when you were barely conscious than when you were aware of your surroundings. You behaved similarly to Tyler in fact, minus the age difference. He was a child, you're an adult; the drugs are different, but the reaction is virtually the same. You see, it's not the Amaris' fault that—he told you that part, right? " I nod. "Good. Well, I like to think of my parents as a, um . . . child. A child will grow up regardless as long as they have their necessities. But if you implement certain tics here and a nudge there—you can get a plethora of different combinations. My parents were always abusive, but when they met that family . . . It was like God left my home."

"What happened?" I blurt out while my body automatically inches toward the woman.

"I don't know what they used on him, but I know they found joy in it. It was the tranquilizers, and they—they silenced his mind. I'm a doctor now, and I still can't put my finger on exactly what drug they used. But he wasn't a bad kid—my brother was expressive. He needed to be nurtured, and they hated him for it. They hated all of us for it. I know that my parents were sick but, Arlissa, Tyler isn't. He was a kid, you know? And they were buying these injections from Bruno and Amy to silence him, and it sounds like a conspiracy theory—we know! Trust me, I get it. But it's our life. So I went to get him. What he did was bad, but he was acting out of a place of pain. You know what that's like, don't you?"

I always thought it was heroin that had a tight grip around Xavier's veins. How couldn't I have? It was the only thing that to my knowledge a person would inject to have a good time. But I could have been wrong since the day we met. I never stopped to ask. I never asked him where it came from or how it happened. Or what it was. I never asked about the depths his dad went through to mold him into who Xavier Amari came to be. I never cared.

"Don't you know what it feels like to want someone to pay for hurting you? But that quick lapse of judgment can cost you your life. You could never drive past another sunset again. I don't want that for you. *We* don't want that for you."

My normal "he deserved it" mantra quickly shifts to guilt as a pang in my chest causes me to bend over slightly. Theodora leans forward and grabs my knee with her hand, but it's not the death grip I've become accustomed to. She does it gently and in the same way Ellie used to. It all comes crashing at once. The guilt, the grief, the heaviness of it all. The way she smiled, the way he smelled, the dreams I had of spending more time with her and the child I never had.

I slept for so long because it mimicked the feeling of death. Conjuring up dreams that were so vivid they passed as realistic. But what I woke up to was even crazier than anything I could make up.

"We want you to come because you understand. Your mom was an alcoholic, and your dad suffered from PTSD from serving in the military. So much so that when you lost your sister, no one gave you a leg to stand on."

Breathing becomes difficult as my entire body starts to shake. My brain is on a rampage and breaks me down with every flowing memory. The lines that once blurred between real and fake are now crystal clear and pain-inducing. I need someone to hold me. I wish I could ask her to hold me.

"You lost your faith a long time ago, but we can help you find it."

Hope never existed. Ellie never took on the Chinese food traditions with me that I used to have with Alejandra. We never had that forced bonding moment of giving birth in her bathtub. The weight of being with Christian never lifted off of my shoulders.

"The people you call home have already locked you out of their foundation. There isn't anything to come back to but a lost, confusing, and Godless life. You believe in God, don't you?"

I tremble in her arms and nod aggressively. I was a terrible model, girlfriend, and friend. The fanbase I did have told me I was legendary, but I am only a fraud. I could possibly be better in a new location with a new face. I can stop getting bombarded with unwanted truths that everyone seems to be aware of but me. I am not a good person. I am not a good woman. And I deserve a second chance.

"I do."

"Then receive his blessings with open arms."

Chapter
THIRTY-FOUR

Saturday. Two pills. One itty-bitty cup of water.

I gulp the contents down for the last time. It goes down painlessly and leaves a metallic taste behind. Everyone is going through the motions and following their designated schedules. It isn't often I see an outburst, but I've caught a few—I'm sure I held a record once before. But the longer I sit here, the more the world fades away.

People become blurry, and clear voices become white noise. I know something they don't. It's my last time here.

I often think about the places I've called home. I compare them to the ones that felt like a safe haven and the ones that didn't. Some had bigger foundations, some had weeds in the yard, and one was completely made up. I think about how that home could have been shared with someone like Nina and Nico, but I know now that they never existed.

Actually, as Dr. Ryan described it, they represented people I wish I knew.

I remember the twin bed at my mother's house because she wouldn't empty Samantha's room to give me more space as I got older. I remember the hole I covered with a dresser. It happened when Alejandra and I were hanging out and she slipped, her elbow going straight into the drywall.

To all of the places I've called home from the high-rise condominium to the mini cottage on Amy's property—I wonder what I could have done to keep them. To go back to waking up on my own time and my biggest problem being the entire day passing me by. I don't get that privilege here. I don't get the privilege of a bathroom with a loofah and a sink full of dishes that are only mine and the people I love.

There's no love here. Through my last few days, I've taken in how the nurses are more scared of us than we are of them. I notice how dangerous that is when a patient goes ballistic and the first thing a nurse does is scream for an officer with a baton and a doctor with a large syringe to come quickly. Whether or not it's the appropriate reaction, it's always the first.

I get up from my normal cafeteria table and notice how the ceiling lights seem brighter today. I don't notice the attitudes of the staff as much, and most importantly I don't internalize it. I walk with my head high in my decision and actually share my goal of the day during Goals group. I tell Dr. Fell that I'd like to see the sun today, and hopefully a rainbow. He tells me that I might have some luck with that because it's supposed to rain.

They give us about ten minutes to clean our room and make sure there isn't a pillow out of sight. Not sure what would happen if there was but that's nothing that's my business. I do it with grace and poise. I pick up my pillow and fluff it happily because if everything goes right, I won't have to make another bed that's this dingy ever again.

With every step I take, it feels like a song is playing behind me. It's a sweet song, with a light dance rhythm that gets me through Theodora's fake therapy session. It's like I'm in an episode of that Charlie Brown show where every word sounds like *womp, womp, womp*. My eyes are glued to the window and taking in the trees that dance against the summer breeze. I take in the power lines and the yellow glow on the bright green leaves. I wonder how it'll feel to touch them.

My last daily walk. It's funny how my first and last fall within the same two weeks. I run my fingers against the blades of grass that are still wet from morning dew. Will the grass outside of this gate feel any different? Will the air I breathe be more crisp? I don't know where we're going yet, but if it's Mexico, does the air taste sweeter?

Well, I do know the food is ten times better. Anything is better than the salted orange eggs and wet bacon. I can sit on a beach and eat all of the delicacies Aly would make for me after school or a video shoot. I can't pronounce anything but—

A nurse shouts and runs outside.

There's screaming. I can't make out what it is or who it's from. There are multiple different voices. It's pure chaos. Everyone is out back. The ones who are in the cafeteria with me are all staring without any discretion. We all want to know what's going on.

Another group is having their time outside, but it must be coming to a close. I stay clung to my seat as people come rushing in and out. A few nurses, a doctor, about three guards. Every single one of them is carrying something. Distressed facial expressions wash over everyone. Crocs and black work boots make their way across the dust-covered green flooring.

The glass door swings back open by a nurse in black scrubs. I'm waiting to see who comes out—I'm curious.

The doctor comes out first. His hair is disheveled, and his mouth is wide open. The guards come behind him, escorting a man in a straitjacket like it's a corny Sunday night film. I vaguely remember visions of being in one. I doubt I'll see him again.

Tyler stays close to me during goal wrap-up. Which I think is bothering Fawn, because she's pouting in the distance. My stomach is full from a dry chicken dinner and saltless mashed potatoes. While Dr. Fell speaks, I dig deep into my brain for a whisper from Samantha. I cling on to the idea that she'll steer me in the right direction while I still have the time. But before I know it, I'm being told to go back to my sleeping quarters for the night. I can't call it a room. You have a room in a home—this isn't a home.

I lay my head on the flat pillow and usher in the end of the day. The moonlight shines through my miniature window and reminds me of a time when I could run outside and bask in it if I wanted to. I close my eyes and drift away into a world I know I can't trust—but also can't avoid.

Tomorrow is the day.

Chapter
THIRTY-FIVE

The blaring fire alarm jolts me out of my sleep. The first thing I do is check my window—it's pitch black outside. The moonlight cascades over a small corner of my box, but before my eyes can adjust to that, the blaring intensifies. The hallway goes from its normal dull color to a sea of flashing red.

The commotion made of scared voices in the hall registers after everything visual. My hands weren't shaking, and my heart wasn't beating out of my chest before, but they are now. I swiftly toss my blanket off and run toward my door. I try to peer down the hallway with the limited visibility I have—no one. But I can hear them. I can hear them yelling, but I can't make out what's being said. There are shrieks of pure terror coming from the left and an audible frustrated conversation happening on the right. The door across from me that is usually shut and has another patient that I honestly never paid much attention to is wide open. The room is empty.

The alarm continues to blare, practically shattering my ears at this point. I bang on the door multiple times, losing all control of myself in the process. I bang and kick the glass, but no one comes.

"Hello!" I scream until my lungs give out in a desperate attempt to combat the sound of the alarm. It only intensifies. The sound alone ignites a fire in me. The red that cascades over my surroundings represents urgency—danger. I pull and kick on the locked door about twenty more times. The stubs that once held manicured nails in another life grow tender from all the tension.

"Can someone get me out of here?" I scream again. Heavy boots begin to echo down the hall at a fast pace. I pound on the glass in order to get their attention. He pauses at my door. I recognize him. My eyes drop to the name tag: Robert. I squint. He looks like any random old guy in this lighting. "Hey, can you open the door?"

He frantically looks behind him and almost takes another step forward.

"Please!"

His eyes go over his shoulder again, and he jogs in place for a few seconds. Finally, he reaches for his key ring and tries to find the one to open my door. I press on the glass desperately. But it's as I'm focusing on the million silver and bronze keys that I smell the smoke.

"Is . . . Is it on fire? Is everything on fucking fire?" I shout. But my screaming only startles him. The assortment of metal drops to the floor, and my anxiety shoots through the roof. "Pick it up!"

The man gulps and holds his keycard tight in his left

hand before running off without another comment. My heart sinks into my stomach as a thick smog begins to hover right under the ceiling.

"Help me! Somebody help me!" I shout until my lungs burn. Hot tears fall down my cheeks as I bang on the door while my knuckles turn tender. The loud thud of my fists is no match for the alarm.

I can't get out. The keys remain on the floor like they're taunting me. One large sheet of heavy glass stands in between me and the exit that I'm sure isn't too far away. My chest feels tight, and the smoke fills my nostrils as it seeps through the air vents. I'm going to die here. In the worst way possible.

I look to see if my window opens—nothing. I look around the space for something, anything to throw to shatter the window. Nothing. Everything is too soft or too heavy for me to carry. I gulp hard and run my fingers through my loose braids. My feet take a few steps back until I bump into the brick wall. The smoke thickens. The alarm roars. The keys are only a few feet away. Sweat beads fall off of my forehead as I inhale more smoke. There is nothing I can do.

A loud thud followed by a groan alerts me to someone down the hall. I can't give up yet. "Hello?" I attempt to shout, but it's interrupted by a cough. "I'm—I'm in here!" My voice is hoarse, but it does its best to carry through the halls.

"There you are. Can you believe I forgot where your room was? I am a mess tonight. I sincerely apologize," Tyler says as he bends down to pick up the keys. "Idiot. I can't believe he wasn't even going to *try* to get you out. The fire won't even spread that fast. Ridiculous." He's fine. He's not struggling to breathe like I am because there's a mask over his face. The only reason I recognize him is the mop-like hair sitting on top of his head. Well, that and his insanely hairy hands. His hands. There's blood on them.

Tyler notices where my stinging eyes fall and wipes his hands on his jeans and then continues to unlock the door. Once I hear the click, my limbs push me outside of the room and into his grasp. I cough once—then three more times. Inhaling becomes more painful than exhaling.

"I—I need to get out of here."

"Yeah, yeah. We know," he mutters and bends down a bit before hiking me over his shoulders.

I allow it to happen as I dangle around his neck. I try to keep my eyes open, but even that proves to be painful. He walks a few steps and then kicks open the door to reveal a stairway. It's cold in here. The fire hasn't touched it yet. Tired eyelids peer open and try to take in some fresh air, but as we head down the stairs, the body of Robert lies idly on the first six or so steps. Tyler doesn't say a word; he just moves over far enough to not step on the body but also not too far that my feet knock against the railing. I lift my head up the best I can in its heavy state, only to see a pool of blood expanding from his.

Tyler remains silent until we're down to what looks like the first floor. I don't remember seeing this back exit before. I don't remember being here at all.

He stops in his tracks. "Can you walk? No offense, but you're kind of heavy."

"Yeah . . ." I mumble loud enough that the alarm doesn't mask the sound of my voice.

He bends down and lets my bare feet hit the cold stone floor. There's an abandoned desk where I'm sure some kind of nurse or receptionist would sit. The door is ajar, but I can't see if there's anyone out there. The sound of sirens comes into play, and Tyler quickly grabs my hand.

"This way," he calmly commands but doesn't allow me to take a step before he's dragging me down a series of halls.

I frantically look up at the ceiling for any sign of smoke—nothing. The alarm becomes a simple sound that is just a part of the moment now. My lungs are still scratchy, but I swallow hard as I take quick steps through the floor that's still surprisingly cold. How is it so empty already?

The sirens sound closer even though we're far from the front door now. Tyler makes a sharp left and stops. He's panting and presses his back against the wall and listens closely. I can hear heavy stomps entering the building and—

"We'll search the premises, see if there's anyone that hasn't made it out yet," a deep voice roars. "Be careful. The building is already beginning to fall."

"What is going on?" I whisper.

He waves me off and remains silent. The footsteps sound like they're coming toward us now. Maybe three, four people. My own emotions are at a standstill while I try desperately to understand what's going on. I was just asleep a couple of minutes ago. I don't know what time it is or where I'm going, I just know this person is here and taking me—somewhere. Is this part of the plan? Was I going to be a body on the staircase if I decided not to go? Where is everyone else?

The rhythmic thud that the boots created begins to fade in another direction. Without notice, Tyler grabs my hand again and pulls me down the hall until we get to a single gray door with a silver bar across it that you use to push it open. He knocks on it three times and waits.

"How do you know the police aren't out there?" I spit out as I hold my hands together to stop them from trembling.

"I know," is all he says before knocking three more times. A rumbling sound comes from above us, and for once he looks up with worry in his eyes.

"How do you—"

The immense ceiling light disconnects and slams against the wall. I jump out of the way and into the nearest corner. Shock fills my features as singed tiles and wiring fall to the ground. The same heat that caressed my skin from the floors above is here now. My heart rate increases as the sound of burning materials becomes too overbearing to ignore—even with the plethora of alarms. The orange-and-red flames dance on the wires and spread right in front of me. My eyes widen and my pupils dilate while I take it in. The fire has arrived on the first floor.

"Tyler . . ." I choke.

"I know. Calm down." His voice shakes slightly, like for the first time he has something to be afraid of. Like something isn't going right. He bangs on the door several more times and gives it a good kick in between knocks. The fire near us continues to grow. I can't look away from it. It starts with engulfing the light fixture whose bulbs are exploding and causing me to shield my body from stray glass. If I listen, I can hear people screaming upstairs—people who didn't make it down.

He keeps banging.

The fire then engulfs the bulletin board that I never looked at until now. I can't tell you what was hung there because almost all of it is burning to pieces. It's getting closer. He shields his mouth in his elbow and doesn't look back at me once. As the smoke fills my lungs, the cough returns with a vengeance. I begin coughing so violently, my lungs scratching with every pressure-filled force of oxygen. I'm sure my throat is bleeding.

He knocks one last time before the door comes swinging open. It's probably a cop. I don't know who Tyler was waiting for, but at this rate we've been left. Where will they take us? Prison? Another hospital? I don't want to be anywhere else. I'm fucking terrified of anywhere else.

"Come on." I can't recognize the voice from behind the door, but Tyler pulls me around and into fresh air. A loud commotion fills my ears—the rest of the ceiling must have fallen.

"Took you long enough," Tyler complains as he wipes ash off of his clothing.

It's Logan. His bald head is covered by a baseball cap that matches his navy-blue uniform. There's no one else out here yet. It's like somehow the commotion is pointed at every part of the building except this one. I turn to the burning building and make out my window. It's engulfed in flames. I can see that much.

I stand there, barefoot in the grass in what I'm sure is the middle of the night. I stare at the trees, an endless array of them that have no clear end. I can touch it if I want to. I can touch them all. I'm free now.

"Hello! Earth to Arlissa!" Tyler whisper-shouts at me.

I check back in to notice Logan with one foot on the pavement and another already heading into the grassy-forest area.

"I'm coming. Sorry," I mumble and follow both men.

"Wait!" The voice is faint, strained, but high-pitched. No one else looks back but me. The woman is bent over. Her normally light hair is covered in ash along with her hands and pajamas.

"Fawn?" I whisper and turn to Tyler, who is pretty much ignoring her and climbing over a bush to follow Logan. "Tyler, that's Fawn!"

"Someone check around back!" a voice shouts from the other side of the building.

"We need to go," Tyler commands in a low tone before making his way safely to the other side.

I find myself standing out in the open in between him and Fawn, who will need help to walk at this point. Adrenaline is the only thing keeping me standing as my eyes tear uncontrollably in reaction to all of the smoke.

"Come on, Arlissa!"

He said she was his girlfriend.

I have maybe ten seconds. Ten to grab her and make it into the forest to get out of here. Worst case scenario: I get caught. I stay here. I go to my trial. Best case scenario: I leave her and end up with a man who has an escalating body count with nothing but guilt weighing on my shoulders.

I can't be that person anymore. That person is afraid of her own shadow.

I bolt to the door and grab onto Fawn. She's heaving. She can't keep her eyes open. The woman drops to her knees, taking in the fresh air the best she can. She's not going to make it. I look over at the two men crouched behind the bushes and trees—they're waiting. But Fawn can't breathe. Her chest is expanding and caving in slowly, like she's barely holding on. I hold the soot-covered woman in my arms and bite on my bottom lip. I can't drag her, and even if I try, she won't make it.

"I-I can't breathe . . ." She forces out.

"It's fine, I got you." I gulp and run my fingers through her hair like getting some of the ash out will help her. "We're over here!" I shout. But before I can get the last word out, the leaves across from me rustle—Logan and Tyler are gone. "We need help! We're here!"

Within moments firefighters, police, and nurses come crowding us. No one puts cuffs on me yet. Instead they pull Fawn out of my arms and place her on a stretcher. They make sure she's strapped in and place an oxygen mask on her face. The firefighters storm the building, and a nurse gently pulls me out of the way.

A million questions are asked in my direction, but I can't answer any of them. I can't move my body or stop my eyes from focusing on one patch of grass in front of me. An EMT comes over and flashes a light at my pupils.

"What's your name?"

"Arlissa Benson."

"Are you a patient?"

"Yes," I say plainly.

Another voice steps in. "How did you get out?"

"I don't know."

"Has anyone left the premises?"

"I don't know."

"Do you know how the fire started?"

"No."

They do a few more of what I assume are routine checks and give me an oxygen mask to place on my face while I sit on the ground. I stare plainly at the scattered people around me. I was free.

"Gather everyone up!"

"Where are we going?" I finally whisper to the nurse hovering over me.

She doesn't answer, instead only softly smiles and passes me some slippers to put on. A nearby guard who escaped the fire slaps some cold cuffs on my wrists before heading to the next patient. She then guides me to a large bus that other patients are boarding.

I was free.

I'm placed in a window seat and watch as the flames are being put out by maybe twenty firefighters. It's not moving, still growing. The building begins to crumble, and debris of all kinds falls to the ground. The bus is filled with patients. Some I've seen before, some I haven't. From the window I can see them loading Fawn's stretcher into the back of an ambulance. She's okay. And I'm not free.

I look at the back of the seat in front of me, where a small rainbow sticker is placed. Its edges are black, from the time the sticker has spent here, I'm sure. But the colors are just as vibrant. Red, like the fire that's searing the place I only just started to get used to. Orange, like the sweater Tyler wore. Yellow, like the sunlight I happened to forget about. Green, like the grass I took for granted. Blue and the sadness it represents that comforts me in these gray-scale moments. Purple, like the bruises that used to form on my body when Xavier overreacted. Indigo, Samantha's favorite color.

I'd like to find new associations for these colors. I'd like a second chance. I'd like to be free.

THANK YOU FOR READING

PLEASE LEAVE A REVIEW ON AMAZON

WWW.GODDESSABROUETTE.COM

Instagram: @goddessabrouettebooks

TikTok: @thegoddessarianna

ACKNOWLEDGEMENTS

Thank you to my loving and supportive family. You might not always get where I'm going with things but you trust me to go anyway and that means more than you know. Mom, JR, Lourdes, Hendrix, Robert, and Ashley! You all have helped me finish this project in one way or another whether you know it or not. Thank you to my friends; Serenity, Sean, and Jean. We've been here before and you all have proven to be rocks for me through all my rants, raves, and idea changes.

Thank you to the wonderful team at Enchanted Ink Publishing for helping this book come alive once again. From your beautiful cover work to your copy editing and formatting. I have gone back to you guys again and again and will continue to do so.

Thank you to my job for not only giving me my first position at a Marketing Agency, but allowing me to be an author as well. From putting my book signing flyers up to letting me whine about the writing deadlines I put on myself; you've helped a bunch. I never expected to be able to practice the arts while also living my dream in the business world as well. You have taught me that it never has to be one or the other. Which reminds me! Thank you to my team! Miranda, Mara, Rob, Sarah, Melissa, GZ, and Dave. You guys were so supportive from the first day we met, I cried a lot about it.

This book is dedicated to my late Godmother, Kashola. I was almost finished with my first draft when she left this physical world. Yet, I feel like she helped me finish it. So thank you. This book is also dedicated to Ashley, who in a way inspired the ending. You have shown me what strength really is and I wanted to embody that in a way Arlissa would. Which, let's be real, isn't the best way but she tries her best. Thank you for being my first and only big sister. Never forget I'm a phone call away. Lastly, it's also dedicated to my late cat; Tom, who also passed away in December of 2021. The pet that I swore was a human and watched me write everyday for years from middle school to high school. I'm eternally grateful for every moment I had with you. Thank you to Kashola and Tom for giving December a new meaning.

Born in The Bronx, New York, Goddess Arianna Brouette always found herself immersed in a fantasy world in order to see something other than the bustling city streets. In fact, she won two poetry awards gifted to her by New York City in middle school. After that, she spent almost a decade focused on character development by writing on Tumblr. After moving to Virginia, she majored in Business at Bridgewater College and was heavily involved in their theater department doing hair and makeup for various plays. But despite all of this, she wanted to go back to writing full-length stories and started her journey as an author.

CPSIA information can be obtained
at www.ICGtesting.com
Printed in the USA
BVHW081055230123
656900BV00003B/199